When the
Heavens
Smiled

When the Heavens Smiled

A heart-stopping, mystic tale of love

Ritesh Arora

Srishti
PUBLISHERS & DISTRIBUTORS

Srishti Publishers & Distributors
Registered Office: N-16, C.R. Park
New Delhi – 110 019
Corporate Office: 212A, Peacock Lane
Shahpur Jat, New Delhi – 110 049
editorial@srishtipublishers.com

First published by
Srishti Publishers & Distributors in 2015

10 9 8 7 6 5 4 3 2 1

Goodbyes are only for those who love with their eyes. Because for those who love with heart and soul there is no such thing as separation.

— *Rumi*

Acknowledgements

⌘

This novel is dedicated to my father (Om Prakash Arora) who would have been proud to see this day.

To my mother (Saroj Arora) who has raised me despite all odds.

My wife (Monica Arora) who has been my partner in reviews and late night story narration sessions.

My son (Aayush Arora) whose giggles and endless energy have motivated me to continue writing in late nights.

My sister (Jasmin Sehgal) who believed in me and always encouraged me to carve out my own path in life.

To my in-laws (Surinder Kumar Kapoor & Sushma Kapoor) and my brother-in-law (Vikrant Kapoor) for their constant motivation.

My sincere thanks to Govind Seshadri who taught me that the art of living is actually the art of giving.

To Diya Bhatia and Surya Sharma whose meticulous reviews have made this book what it is today.

Finally, to all my readers who decided to purchase my book and to Srishti Publishers, who showed faith in my script and agreed to publish and distribute it.

You can send in your feedback about the book at xmlatitsbest@gmail.com or on my official Facebook fan page (Ritesh Arora *or* WhentheHeavensSmiled).

From the Mughal Capital
to the City of Joy

⌘

2013

My final year in engineering college was the year when I appeared for interviews for campus placements. The first three years of engineering college are cake and ale when one can have boisterous fun, while the final year is the year you're given a chance to prove your mettle in the campus interviews. Getting a job through a campus interview is a matter of pride for not only the engineering students, but also for their parents. My class, like all other classes, had a mixed bag of students – intelligent, average and the backbenchers. I was amongst one of the sharper minds in my branch of Electrical Engineering. Soon, the day of the campus interviews arrived and various companies – multinational and domestic – formed the beeline to our college to recruit bright minds. The placement interviews had a formal dress code and my mother had bought me a navy blue coloured suit, with an off white shirt and yellow tie. As they say, dress shabbily and they remember the dress; dress impeccably and they remember you. The campus interview in total had three rounds – a written exam, followed by a group discussion and finally an in-person interview with company officials. I finished the written exam fifteen minutes before time and scored forty-five out of fifty, which was good enough to take me to the second round. But, things are never easy for more than a minute. Before I could breathe a sigh of relief, my name was called out loud for the second round – the group discussion. My group was given the topic 'Does talent matter or hard work?' and one could either support or oppose it. I not only argued in favour of hard work but smashed the arguments of other contestants mercilessly. I felt sorry for them but one shouldn't mix emotions with duty. Good news was soon to follow. Going strong, I was through to the final round – the in-person interview with a company called NetCon Consulting. It was one of the companies that I had opted to appear for in the campus interview.

In the final round, the panelists asked me varied questions on topics ranging from Applied Physics to Thermodynamics and I answered almost all of them with ease.

From my childhood, I had this unusual knack of sticking to a problem and not giving up until its logical end was achieved. This trait of mine would enable me to take on some of the biggest challenges that one could ever face in one's life. I will show you how destiny started playing the dice with me – what I did and how I did it. When I look back at it now, I get a Tom Sawyer kind of feeling. I will write about that in a minute, but let us stick to the campus selection part, which was a mixed bag of fun, hard work, and a bit of luck.

"Mr Sarthak Arora, without a doubt, your previous year's mark sheets and results of the first two rounds are impressive," said one of the panelists.

His desk had a name plate bearing a name 'Ramaprasad Ramamurthy, NetCon Consulting'.

I nodded, acknowledging his feedback. Different shades of grey hair on his head indicated that he was a senior employee in NetCon, likely in his early forties. Such kind words from a senior person like him were an honour.

"I, however, noticed that your attendance in the final year is a meagre forty-five percent? What happened, boring professors?" asked a grinning Ram as he highlighted my attendance records with a blue marker.

In my final year I had become addicted to playing table tennis with my roommates, Raja and Ankur, and ended up bunking more than half the classes. You know, walk in the company of the wise and you will be wise; walk with bums and you shall suffer harm. I couldn't tell Ram the truth. I didn't even try to give an excuse. Your well-wishers don't need them and your foes won't believe them.

"Ram, most of the guys tire of a lecture in ten minutes, clever ones in five minutes and smart ones will never go to the lecture!" I said playing the humour card. No humorist is under any obligation to provide answers.

Ram smiled at my answer.

"Smart answer! I like your wit, but a job at NetCon is no beer and skittles. It not only needs street smartness but also hard work and intelligence. Nonetheless, let me ask you one final question before we close this interview," he said with that cunning smile on his face which intuited me that something tricky was on my way.

"There is a woman, who shoots her husband. Then she holds him under water for minutes. Finally, she hangs him, but minutes later they go out for a dinner together. How do you think this is possible?" asked Ram, handing me a paper that had the puzzle written on it.

"Since morning, none of the candidates who made it till this round have been able to answer this. Trust me, if you crack this or even come close to solving this, you stand a chance. You have got exactly sixty seconds to solve this and your time starts now!" Ram said with conviction in his voice and stared at his watch.

He had offered me a make or break deal. A right answer could reward me with a job and a wrong one could blow it all up. I read the puzzle again; the dots, however, were not getting connected. Well, dots are never supposed to connect so easily in life and that is why life is nothing but a puzzle. I started thinking out of the box and focused hard. It occurred to me that my best side was at work and soon the clarity came. In the puzzle, the word 'shoot' had been used differently. It wasn't 'shoot' with respect to a gun, but that of a camera.

"Ram, the woman was a photographer. She shot a picture of her husband, developed the film and hung it up to dry. Then both of them went out for dinner," I said confidently.

I knew that my answer was right and I looked at my watch: the seconds hand showed forty-five seconds, a full fifteen seconds short of Ram's deadline. I had got the better of Ram in his challenge. The feeling was ripping. It was like for the first time a child beat an adult at chess. Ram's expressions were a treat to watch and 'awesome' was written all over his face.

"Excellent, Sarthak! You are the first person in the campus interview to solve this. Whether we select you or not is a different story, but I like your speed and confidence!" he said nodding his head in appreciation. "Thank you for your time. We will evaluate your performance and revert. Is that okay?" he said placing the phone on the desk.

I got up from the chair, shook hands with him and gently placed the chair back. I looked at him and his body language was oozing positivity. Human race had body language before it had speech, and eighty percent of what you understand in a conversation is read through the body, not through the words. While coming out of the hall I did not know whether I had made it, but I felt strangely confident. My mother was waiting outside the hall with bated breath.

"How did the interview go?" she asked, handing me a can of coke.

"I think it went well. I almost answered everything, literally. Hopefully the deal should be in the can." I said sipping the coke, slightly nervous from within. I think it's healthy for a person to be nervous. It means you care, that you have worked hard and given your best performance.

In the campus interview, my mother had accompanied me, but not my father. Truth be told, my father was missing since my childhood. Though he was the one to bring home the bacon, he was more engrossed in his work and club life than in his family. Mom and I had become used to his 'deficiency' all these years and hence his presence or absence made little or no difference. I looked at my mom; she had her fingers crossed in hope. As they say, God cannot be everywhere and therefore he made mothers.

It was now afternoon when the final selection results were to be announced. All the students who appeared in the campus interview had gathered outside the college auditorium, waiting for the lucky call. It was a restless moment for all, as the coordinator had informed that only twenty-five students out of one hundred seventy-five had been selected. The placement coordinator, with a microphone in his hand, had started calling out the names of the students who were selected by different companies. A few Atuls, Mohits and Amits were called out, I wasn't. Not yet.

"Jitin Kumar, Rakesh Bhardwaj, Anshul Brar, Hemant Ahuja…," shouted the coordinator.

Shortly, the count of names that the coordinator was calling appeared to be more than twenty. With the sinking feeling that the list would be over soon without my name being announced, I wondered what could have gone wrong. I had done well in all the rounds and had even solved the puzzle thrown by Ram. I looked at my mom, and she was a bag of nerves with every name that was being called out.

"Sarthak Arora," shouted the coordinator, "go to table number six in auditorium two, and meet the NetCon Consulting team."

This was awesome and brought a ray of sunshine. I looked back at my mother and she had tears in her eyes – tears of joy. I had come a long way to see this day in my life. I ran towards auditorium two where executives from various companies were seated and were rolling out offers to the selected candidates. NetCon Consulting was on table number six. I walked towards the table and saw Ram sitting with a good looking girl dressed in black formals. I guessed that she was from the HR department of NetCon Consulting.

"Congratulations, Sarthak! I am pleased to inform you that NetCon Consulting has selected you for a job. Your performance in all three rounds was exceptional among all the candidates we interviewed," said Ram affirmatively while shaking my hands.

"Your place of work will be our Kolkata office. Along with the other selected candidates, you would need to join by September this year. I would like you to work with a manager named Rajan, who looks after our UK team for all Java projects. Other than the project, if you need any help, Aparna will be your point of HR contact in Kolkata," said Ram, indicating towards the unquestionably eyeful girl sitting next to him.

"Many thanks Ram, it was my pleasure too, and I look forward to working with NetCon," I said shaking hands with him.

"Thank you Aparna, for the opportunity," I said as I shook hands with her longer than I should have. Aparna simply smiled.

"Ram told me about how well you answered the questions, and especially the puzzle. We have lots of intelligent guys like you in our company and you will get to meet them once you are in Kolkata," she said, talking sweetly with a grin. I think human resource people are born with sugar candies in their mouths.

"I will call you in the second week of June to brief you on the joining formalities and the documents that you'll need to bring along," she said with that extra display of halo white teeth. I had no clue why she was working for NetCon when she could have been a perfect model for Colgate or Pepsodent toothpaste with that smile.

"Sure," I said returning the smile, realizing that I was paying more attention to her looks than what she was saying. Ram in the meantime handed me an envelope that had the offer letter, and holding that felt magical.

"Here is your offer letter. Go through it, it has two copies; you can keep one and return the second one to me after signing the last page," said Ram.

Nothing succeeds like success. I hurriedly opened it up and it had a bunch of pages describing various company clauses and agreements. I quickly skimmed through it to the end but one page read 'CTC (Cost to the company)' as '520,000 per annum' and that would mean a take home salary of twenty-five thousand per month. Knowledge may make one laugh, but money makes one dance. I read that page twice and was on cloud nine.

"All the best, Sarthak and we will see you soon in Kolkata!" he said, again shaking hands with me. I used this parting opportunity to shake hands with Aparna once again. Boys will always be boys! I signed the copy of the offer letter, handed one copy to Aparna, kept the other with me, and came out of the hall dancing, waving the letter up. I had won the day for myself and my parents, my mother to be specific.

"It is NetCon Consulting, Kolkata, and my salary will be twenty-five thousand per month," I said, over the moon, hugging my mother.

Hearing this, she was delighted but I felt her tears on my shoulders. All that I was going to be or I hoped to be, I owed it to my mother.

"With the first month's salary, I will get a new air conditioner for your room," I said looking at her. The only air conditioner that we had at home was broken and Delhi summers without an AC are intolerable.

I soon came to know that I had bagged the highest salary package among all the selected students. My mother and I celebrated this news with tea, pakoras and gulab jamun in the college canteen. So engrossed we had been celebrating that the clock had raced to seven in the evening and the stars were out in the sky. It was time to go home.

"Taxi!" I shouted, spotting a vacant taxi going in the opposite direction. Hearing my shout, the taxi took a u-turn and came towards us.

"South Extension, Part II. Not very far off from here," I said in a single breath.

Soon we were home and my mother opened the lock as my father was not at home as usual.

"This bitch of a campus placement sucked the last drop of life out of me. For the whole day, I have been writing exams and giving answers to people who have lesser IQ than me!" I said throwing the bag that had my previous semester mark sheets on the sofa.

"From where have you picked up this crappy language, Sarthak?" she asked in astonishment, entering the kitchen but giving back looks. I kept mum and tried looking elsewhere. Before I could ask for food she had realized that I would be hungry after the day-long interviews. She started to make an omelette for me. A mother is after all a mother who understands what a child does not say.

"Ma, paranthas too...without butter! Butter is a son of a bitch, full of bloody cholesterol," I said trying to duck her question but still ended up using bad words. She gave me those looks again because of my language, but this time I reverted with a sorry gesture quickly. How could I tell her that this was the entry level language in college and would only get worse!

"I am glad that you've got a good job, but isn't Kolkata too far and culturally different too? I am little worried...," she said from inside the kitchen, stuffing potatoes inside the parantha. While there was a nice aroma arising from the kitchen, her voice had a note of unease.

"Kolkata is just an overnight journey, Mom, and I can come home every fortnight," I said trying to assure her.

"You know, I had an intuition that you would be getting a job soon and therefore, I already bought two shirts for you.

You could wear these in your new company. Good clothes help in creating good impressions," she said, coming out of kitchen and taking out two new Louis Philippe shirts for me from her almirah.

While my dad had no clue about my new job, my mother had already planned things in advance. Someone has said it right that most of all the other beautiful things in life come in twos, threes, dozens and hundreds, but there is only one mother in the whole world.

"Sarthak, where are you going to live in Kolkata? How are you going to manage your food?" she asked going inside the kitchen and tossing the omelette. She had too many questions, but as a mother, she had a right to ask them.

"The company guy told me that they would put me up in a company guesthouse for the first two weeks. He also said the guesthouse would have food joints nearby. After two weeks, I can find accommodation. Don't worry Ma; you know Kolkata is a city for foodies!" I said trying to soothe her worries, while playing with the TV remote.

Sony Max was showing highlights of IPL 6 Kings XI Punjab vs Chennai Super Kings. Chennai was batting and Dhoni was smashing the ball everywhere on the field.

"Avoid eating food outside and try to get an apartment as soon as you can. Find a good Bengali cook who can prepare meals at home for you," she said, instructing me from the kitchen. The aroma from the kitchen signalled that the omelette and paranthas were ready to be served.

"Paranthas are the greatest food that we mortals know of," I said after taking the first bite. When you know that home cooked food won't be available in the next few months, your taste buds start appreciating it more. I finished the omelette and parantha and went out to play table tennis in the society club where I was hailed as a local hero.

✠

The next two months passed in no time; my final semester results were out too. I had stood second in my electrical branch and third overall in college with eighty-one percent marks. September had started and it was time to leave for Kolkata to join NetCon Consulting. It was a Friday and I had tickets for the train to Kolkata on Sunday, that would depart from the New Delhi railway station.

"You are being so carefree! You haven't even started packing yet. Do you realize that you have a train journey in the next forty-eight hours?" she said, placing my ironed clothes inside my suitcase.

"Once your physics professor from first year of college had called me and complained that you weren't serious about your studies. He grumbled about your addiction to table tennis. He also confidently said that you wouldn't even pass in your first semester. That night, I was so tense and couldn't sleep, you know!" she said, continuing to pack but looking at me and smiling.

"Oh that Monologue Nattu! Sorry, I mean physics professor Mr. Natarajan! You don't know anything about him. Every student hated him and he used to have an awful attendance in his lectures," I said.

"Awful attendance…? But why…?" she asked, fazed.

"Firstly, he was a bore till death and secondly, highly myopic – you know those who have a problem seeing things that are at a distance. Students would just slip out of his class in front of him and he would never come to know. Once I clicked his picture while he was lecturing the empty benches in the second semester," I said grinning.

"That is very bad, Sarthak. You should give a lot of respect to your professors. By the way, what did you do with that snap?" she asked inquisitively.

"What else? Posted it on Facebook from a fake profile! The number of 'likes' that it got were more than the votes that Narendra Modi got in the Gujarat elections," I said, untying my shoe laces and smirking.

"My God! You shouldn't do such things to your professors. You, in fact, should be thankful to them as what you are today is because of them. Lately, I have been observing that you have started thinking too much about yourself. You seem really self-involved," she said switching on the iron.

"In fact, I think very less of what I actually am," I said.

Self-praise is no recommendation but both of us had a hearty laugh. I joined her in packing and started to iron my clothes, while she continued to place them neatly in my suitcase.

I had my train reservation in the Duronto Express on Sunday from New Delhi railway station to Sealdah station in Kolkata. The New Delhi railway station brings people from all walks of life momentarily together, travelling to various parts of the country. Trains coming and leaving the platform teach you an important lesson of life – keep moving. Raja and Ankur, my roommates in engineering college were from Kolkata and we had planned to meet up at Sealdah station in Kolkata upon my arrival. Though they were my buddies, they weren't that lucky in getting jobs during the campus placements. I was a Punjabi from a service class background, Raja a Bengali, the only son in an army family, and Ankur a Marwari hailing from a business family that exported leather goods. We were all misfits in our different ways, but our differences strangely fitted well in our friendship. We were roommates in college and now were going to be in the same city. It was probably scripted in our destiny. The trio of Raja, Ankur and I would become important characters in playing dice with the script of destiny of an important person whom I will introduce shortly. I will talk about the girl I fell in love with, the trying times and how great principles emerged out of the entire episode.

The reservation chart was pasted on the platform fifteen minutes prior to the train's arrival, that read 'Sarthak Arora, Age 22, berth number 37 A, AC second class.'

"All set Mom! Thank you for all your help in packing. I will call you once I reach Kolkata," I said, hugging her, and rushed towards my compartment as my watch showed that only ten minutes remained for the departure.

"Call me in once during the journey as well, and once you reach Kolkata. Don't accept anything to eat from strangers," she said getting slightly nervous.

The joys of parents are secret and so are their fears; they cannot utter one, nor can they utter the other. It was for the first time that I was going to be out of Delhi and on my own.

I had an upper berth and that was good in the sense that it gives you your much needed privacy. I placed my luggage beneath the lower berth, tied it with a chain and swiftly climbed up. I took my iPhone out, plugged in the earphones and started listening to music. While listening to the music, I noticed that a middle-aged couple was sitting on the lower berth opposite to me. My iPhone wasn't charged well and its battery was alarming an alert. I stopped the music and took off my earphones. With the music stopped, I was able to hear their conversation and understood that they were from Ballygunge, a place in Central Kolkata. The Bengali man was a six feet plus stalwart and I kept wondering how he would fit in his berth, though it was none of my business. Opposite to him was his wife, wearing a black sari with a big red coloured bindi. Soon afterwards, the train picked up speed. I did not know when I fell asleep. Shortly it occurred to me that the train had come to a halt and the surroundings had become raucous. I peeped from the corner of my blanket and realised that Kolkata, the 'City of Joy', had arrived.

"Chalo chalo... Kolkata *aeshe gailo, dada* (Kolkata has come, brother). Should I pick up your luggage? I will not charge much," said one of the coolies wearing a red kurta and a white dhoti, almost picking up my luggage.

"Don't touch it! I will manage it myself. It is just one bag anyway," I said, swiftly coming down from my berth.

I unlocked the chain and dragged the suitcase towards the compartment door. The signboard in front of me had 'Welcome to Kolkata' written on it. Standing at the door of my compartment, I took a deep breath of the air and felt an immediate connection with the city and thought, *I am where I ought to be.*

I got down from the train and looked for Ankur and Raja who were supposed to be in front of the compartment but were nowhere in sight. I was a little surprised as I couldn't find them anywhere on the platform. They were of course absentminded and bums at times, but surely they couldn't have forgotten my arrival time. I dialled Raja's number but he didn't pick up.

"Ladies and gentleman, please welcome Mr Sarthak Arora from Delhi! Now that he is in Kolkata, in no time it will become a sin city!" said someone almost singing from the back. I felt a hand hugging me and a leg kicking me from behind. It was none other than gung–ho Raja and Ankur and it was magical seeing them again after college. Someone has said it right – 'great friends are hard to find, difficult to forget and impossible to leave.'

"Guys, now that our pal has arrived in the city, shall we go for our 'adda'?" Ankur said. By 'adda', he meant booze at ten in the morning.

"Dude, can I take a nap in my guesthouse and then go out to paint the town red?" I said. I had hardly completed my statement and I saw a spark in Raja's eyes.

"Sure, dude! Let us plan to meet at Trincas in the evening – booze, live music and boneless chicken. I don't need anything or anyone else in life," said a visibly euphoric Raja.

Ankur dialled a prepaid Innova that arrived in no time. I put my luggage inside the cab and sat. Raja and Ankur followed it on their bike that oozed more smoke than a steam engine. Soon we were at my company's guesthouse in Rajarhat, an area close to my office.

"Dude, you go and sleep, we will pick you up from here at seven sharp. Ankur and I are skipping our lunch so that we can have endless pieces of chicken kebabs at Trincas. Sounds like a plan?" Raja said, sounding excited.

I nodded and they left. A guesthouse boy carried my luggage to room number 507. I fell off to sleep as soon as I hit bed.

I was hardly few hours into my sleep, when I realized that someone was banging my room's door even when there was a doorbell outside. With sleepy eyes, I looked at my watch and it showed six thirty in the evening. No brainer to guess that it couldn't have been any one else other than those dogs. They were at my place half an hour before the agreed time. If they had shown this kind of discipline in college, they would have made it to Harvard or Stanford.

"Taxi!" Raja shouted and soon the three of us were on our way to Trincas – a sumptuous wine and dine place located in Park Street, the heart of the city. We began our night with vodka shots, to be followed with Teacher's whisky and finally gin with some chicken kebabs. The live music band was singing a mix of romantic English, Hindi and Bengali numbers. Amidst the wine, food and groove with music, the clock had raced to eleven.

"Sir, the bar will be closed in a few minutes. Do you want anything else?" asked the waiter humbly.

I paid the bill and we hired a yellow cab outside Trincas. On the way we stopped by a local wine shop to buy some more booze to celebrate our newly found independence.

"Alcohol might be man's worst enemy, but the Bible says love your enemy!" said Raja opening up the bottle of Kingfisher beer while the cab was crossing Science City. Boozing continued in the taxi and by the time we reached my guesthouse, Ankur and Raja were so tipsy that if their parents saw them in this moon-eyed condition, they would have disowned them. The only option left for them was to spend the night at my guesthouse.

"That's my guesthouse. Please stop here," I instructed the cab driver who immediately applied the brakes.

Ankur, who appeared slightly better and in control than the both of us, paid the driver and then dragged Raja and me out of cab one by one. He took out the room keys from my pocket, but instead of going towards the guesthouse, went towards a lamp post nearby and tried fitting in the keys in vain there.

The guesthouse's Nepali security guard who was watching from a distance, said in amusement, "It is no use sir, no one is at home!"

"That is precisely where you are wrong," fuddled Ankur, "see there is a light on upstairs."

The cat was out of the bag and it was obvious for the guard to guess what we were up to. He, however, was kind enough to take us to my room upstairs through the lift. All of us slept like babies in my room with Raja on my bed, Ankur on the carpet, and I, upon whose name the room was booked, on the dining table.

Having drunk like a fish, I finally woke up at two in the afternoon. Raja and Ankur must have left for their homes as they were nowhere around. Jesus! I was supposed to be in office by nine in the morning for my joining formalities. Someone has said it right, you never run out of things that can go wrong.

I quickly changed to my office formals, got hold of a taxi and by the time I reached office, it was 3.00 p.m. I was supposed to meet Aparna for my introduction to my new project manager Rajan at 9.00 a.m. Not only was I six hours late, but also had blood-shot eyes from the previous night's drinking spree.

"There is no afternoon shift in NetCon! Our office starts at nine on weekdays!" Aparna said, getting ratty. She was talking salty unlike the sweet, easy on the eye babe in the campus interview.

"Aparna, I've got an upset stomach since last night. I think the food that was served in the train was stale. I have been feeling terrible ever since," I said, lying and trying to look like a patient suffering from a bout of week-long diarrhoea.

Hearing this, her expression suddenly changed from not-giving-a-damn to sympathetic. Before she could offer me any consolation or say anything further about my meeting with Rajan, my phone buzzed and it was Ankur on the line. Why was this bugger calling at this hour? From the heavy drinking the previous night, my mind was still fuzzy till then and I accidently pressed the speaker button. If there is a worse time for anything to go wrong, it will go wrong then.

"Where the hell are you dude? We are waiting outside your office for the last one hour. Didn't you say that it would be some useless orientation training and you would sneak out by lunch time and we would all go to drink at Soho? It is three already, asshole!" Ankur said on the speaker phone and Aparna looked at me in disbelief. Soho is a tip top lounge at Minto Park in Kolkata.

"Sorry…wrong number!" I said swiftly cutting the line. Aparna had heard loud and clear what Ankur had said on the speaker phone. On that day, I learnt that if you perceive that a thing can go wrong in four possible ways and circumvent them, then a fifth unprepared for way will promptly develop. I could see that Aparna had realized that I was trying to pull wool over her eyes. I was caught red handed in front of the authority that employs as well as terminates people's jobs in the company.

"Must be a wrong number, no?!" said Aparna grinning. I couldn't guess whether she was being sarcastic or had believed that it was indeed a wrong number.

"Train journeys can be bothersome at times but what to do, new joinees as per company policy have to travel by train only. You go home, get some rest and come back fresh tomorrow and I will introduce you to Rajan, your new project manager," she said with a mischievous beam. Though I nodded, I was still feeling embarrassed within. The accidental press of the speaker button had dented my perception of being intelligent in the eyes of Aparna. Feeling gutted, I started walking slowly out of her cubicle.

"Once you are done with Soho today, try Tantra, another popular night club in town. I keep getting complimentary passes for it, and next time, I will give them to you. Have fun with your friends who are waiting outside!" she said with a smile on her face. I looked back and smiled too.

"Sorry boss... Just drank a bit too much last night, but I promise to be on time tomorrow to meet Rajan!" I said, confessing and apologizing.

"Don't worry too much; Rajan is also not in today!" she said, smiling, and I heaved a sigh of relief. God is kind.

"See you tomorrow then," she said, resuming her work.

Sometime accidents in life build everlasting relationships. Aparna has been a great buddy till date.

I came down to the visitor's parking where Ankur and Raja were waiting on their bike, pulling the accelerator and making that throttling sound.

"Bastards, you will get me killed one day! The HR lady heard what all you said on the phone," I said hopping mad at Ankur's language on the phone.

"I have heard that the NetCon HR is a babe. Saale, why don't you introduce her to me? I am still single and ready to mingle," said Ankur sitting in the middle and we all laughed. You can't change your past but you can laugh at it for sure.

"Guys control your laughter, you are distracting the captain of the ship," said Raja speeding well above the permissible limit. On the way to Soho, the cops at different places in the city noticed the three of us on a single bike. Raja waved at all of them, and they in-turn acknowledged. The best way to eliminate your enemy is to befriend them. We had reached Soho and another drinking binge was about to begin.

Raja, Ankur and I were great buddies; we always had a plan up the flagpole. Kolkata, a place of bright minds, sumptuous street food, and pretty Bong girls to look at, was the place where we ought to be. In this city of joy, saving any money was out of question and the intent was to blow up the salary before the next month's salary was credited. In the next three months, we watched all movies – Hollywood, Bollywood or Tollywood – and dined at places ranging from street hawkers to pocket pinching restaurants in Park Street, of course, all sponsored by me. There was great magic unfolding in the city and you could smell fun and friendship in the air. The Kolkata chapter was in top gear.

The Bong Connection

⌘

I was entitled to two weeks of free stay in the guesthouse. It had a Nepali cook who would cook mouth-watering dishes for all occupants of the guesthouse. Barring the booze, the guesthouse had all modern amenities of life that bachelors need – a furnished room with an air conditioner, a television, a refrigerator and a double bed. Free things in life don't last for very long and my free days in the guesthouse were up soon. I started searching for a house in the city and settled in a society by the name of Starwood Estate a little away from the city but the facilities in it made up for the distance. It had round the clock security, swimming pools, gymnasiums, a cafeteria, a club house, a movie theatre and of course – good looking Bong girls. The only fly in the ointment was the fact that my landlord, Mr. Roy, was my neighbour. Everything I would say or do was heard by him, as he seemed to have nothing to do being retired and curious. I hated it, wanted to put a blanket on him and kick him. Privacy is not something that we are entitled to, it's an absolute prerequisite for every human being.

Kolkata, the city of joy, has its own pace of life. It does not give a tinker's cuss about show off, businesses or what car your neighbour has, but rather subtly tells you to find pleasures in

21

simple things of life like eating phuchkas in New Market or queuing up at Peter Cat for its delicious chelo kebabs. In three months, we had visited all the happening places in Kolkata and now the quest was on for a new unexplored place.

"Dude, I have been noticing that our friend only takes us to bum places," Ankur said to Raja, obviously hinting at me. It was a bright Sunday morning and Raja, Ankur and I were sipping tea in my apartment.

"Bum places? I thought we had a sumptuous dinner at Flame and Grill last week!" I said, reacting to the false accusation thrown at me.

"I think what he means is that there are a few good places we have not been to. Our highly paid friend is now well-settled in the town and we should check them out," said Raja mediating diplomatically and slowly drinking his tea with a sipping sound.

"Okay...And which are those places if I may ask?" I asked, slightly surprised at what places Raja meant.

"The Grand Vilas is where I would love to go!" said Raja, with a spark in his eyes.

"Have you gone nuts? Of course you are joking, right?!" said Ankur, looking at Raja. The Grand Vilas is one of the luxury five star hotels in Kolkata where the bill does not come in red cents.

"Over my dead body! The Grand Vilas is way beyond our budget. Just to tell you guys, I have been there for company meetings and one time buffet lunch cost two thousand rupees per person. Mind you, taxes are additional!" I reacted to Raja's wasteful suggestion. We three were fit for pocket friendly phuchkas or chelo kebabs at Park Street at the max. But The Grand Vilas? No way!

"Two thousand per person?! What do the dishes contain? Pearl or diamond toppings?" said an astonished Ankur.

There was silence for a while and the only sound in the air was of Raja sipping tea. The plan of lunching at The Grand Vilas was shot down at the outset. Raja's expressions, however, indicated that he had another plan up his sleeve. Confused, Ankur and I looked at one another.

"Guys, we won't go there for lunch, but for coffee. I know someone at The Grand Vilas who can get us a seventy-five percent discount, but only on coffee!" said Raja with conviction in his voice.

"Spend some time sipping coffee at the place of the rich and famous! Good news is that with that discount, the overall bill would come to less than a thousand for all three of us!" continued a buoyant Raja. Having confidence in your word is what makes you sound convincing.

Thousand for three guys would mean three hundred fifty rupees per person. It wasn't that bad a proposal at all. Of course, we could have coffee at such a posh place, but more than that, I could click selfies and post them on Facebook to show off. But as the wise say, there is a flip side to everything that seems great in the first instance. I wanted to know how we could get three coffees at The Grand Vilas at less than one thousand rupees. The devil mostly lies in the details.

"Whom do you know there who can get you a seventy-five percent discount?" I asked, curious. Ten to twenty percent discount is still understandable, but seventy-five percent was too good to be true.

"The owner of The Grand Vilas group of hotels is Raja's chaddi friend," said Ankur, again ridiculing Raja.

"Guys don't bother about counting the trees; just enjoy the fruit! Assume that you have got the discount. Let us plan for The Grand Vilas for today evening," said Raja, easing my tense nerves before I could throw more questions. He appeared supremely confident and there was no point in questioning him further.

The coffee plan appeared robust, at least for the time being. The cornerstone of successful execution was the discount person Raja seemed to know. Little did I know at that point in time that 'the discount person' would shortly become the person with whom I would rejoice; share my joys and my sorrows. Every moment in life has infinite possibilities. Sounds captivating? Stay with me.

"Guys, it is already six now! If you dilly dally any longer, we won't get a place to sit," said Raja, instructing both of us.

"Won't get a seat?! You mean there are people in this city who pay a thousand rupees for one coffee?" asked a flabbergasted Ankur.

"Yes sir, there are. Not everyone in Kolkata has a three digit bank balance like you and me," said an irritated Raja on a turkey question from Ankur. Soon the three of us were on Raja's bike, tricking the traffic cops on our way, and soon reached The Grand Vilas.

The hotel had splendid interiors with huge chandeliers mounted on the ceilings, illuminating the interiors. The hotel walls had fine tapestry and there were designer paintings everywhere. And yes, the hotel appeared crowded from a weekend gathering.

"Follow me guys," said Raja, taking a right turn and walking past a long lobby, and we soon reached the coffee shop of The Grand Vilas. Raja looked supremely confident and there was no point in racking our brains on 'Operation Discount'. The coffee shop had spiffing leather upholstery sofas and our chatting

"Didn't you confidently declare at home that we could assume we have got the discount?" I asked beginning to sweat. Not getting the discount would escalate the bill to more than three thousand bucks!

A flustered Raja swiftly walked to the hotel's front office desk to inquire about the discount person. It was now a contest between Raja coming back with the discount first or waiter coming back with the cookies and the bill. The waiter was not in sight yet, but I saw Raja coming towards us with his head down. His body language no longer had the excitement of free cookies and coffee at The Grand Vilas.

"What happened dude? Did you talk to the discount person?" I asked even though the answer was evident in his body language. I could sense that 'Operation Discount' had gone wrong somewhere.

"The discount person has not been in the office till now and her phone is also unreachable," said Raja in a dampened tone.

Without the discount, the coffee bill was going to be three thousand five hundred. The desire to upload a Facebook selfie in The Grand Vilas had come at an outrageous price. Chance of the bread falling with the buttered side down is directly proportional to the cost of the carpet.

"In short, I think it means that we are royally screwed, right?" asked a rattled Ankur who had probably had twenty of the thirty cookies from the bowl that the waiter gave us.

"Did you check with that discount person to see if she is going to be in the hotel in time?" I asked, spiked up with Raja's terrible planning.

"Yaar, she is here all throughout the week except on Thursdays. Today is Sunday; she was definitely supposed to be here. I have been aware of her working hours for years now. Looks like our stars aren't aligned today," said Raja, trying to blame the stars and attempting to save his ass.

The waiter came back with a speed that was faster than that of light, and with that damn bill in his hand. There was no other escape route except to pay the bill in full. Faking a smile, I took the bill from him. It read 'three thousand four hundred and twenty-six, inclusive of taxes'.

I reluctantly placed my credit card inside the bill folder and handed it to him and he walked towards the billing desk. Shortly, an sms on my phone indicated that the card was swiped and money deducted. Bitch! The world is a dream for the wise, a comedy for the rich and a tragedy for the middle class.

"Sir, I hope that you enjoyed your coffee and will come again soon," said the waiter, handing me the credit card. I faked a smile as I was livid with Raja's poor planning. The credit card was swiped, the money was deducted and therefore there was no point in crying over spilt milk. An important lesson of life that I learnt on that day – if everything seems to be going well, you have obviously overlooked something.

With the coffee shop closed and the coffee plan ending in disaster, it was time to pack up. We had just got up from the table when a honey like voice came from somewhere in the back, "Hey Raja, what are you doing here?"

The three of us turned around only to find an angelic beauty with constellation blue eyes. Elegantly dressed in a brown coloured sari, she was about five feet six inches in height. She had a tapered waist, a gleaming complexion and a pair of arched eyebrows that looked down on sweeping eyelashes. Her delicate ears were framing a button nose. In short, she was God's handwriting.

"Sarangi, it is so amazing to see you here!" said Raja, grinning from ear to ear. Asshole Raja came forward to give her a short hug as well. He bore no sign of depression from the big screw up. The more I came to know of men, the more I loved dogs.

"How come you are here and never told me about your visit to The Grand Vilas?" she asked in a cuckoo like voice that had the chirp, effervescence and curiosity of a child.

"Arre, we came just like that. There wasn't any plan. But I did try to reach you a few minutes back, but your phone was switched off," said Raja spouting a tall story. Raja was obviously yarning but it wasn't his fault. The trouble with women is that if they are good looking, men tend to lose their minds or become first class liars.

"Asshole has shown his true colours seeing a babe!" I murmured. Ankur heard that and tried controlling his creased up laughter. Raja couldn't listen to what I had said, while Sarangi looked confused on seeing Ankur laughing like a drain.

"Guys, let me do the introductions. She is Sarangi, front office manager at The Grand Vilas. And you know what, she was the discount person whom we just missed by a whisker. Would you believe it? Our bad!" said a grinning Raja.

Sarangi had arrived a few seconds after I had paid the bill in full, thanks to Raja's crappy planning. I was of course depressed on spending three thousand five hundred on dogs, but the sight of the cherubic Sarangi was like an ice cube on a burn. It did not cure my wound, but healed it to a large extent. She was easy on the eyes and I unintentionally kept looking at her for more than a few seconds.

"Ahem, Ahem…" said Raja, artificially clearing his throat, indicating that Sarangi was conscious of our gaze.

"Hi, I am Sarthak, Sarthak Arora. I work for NetCon Consulting," I said, introducing myself and extending my hand to the cherubic beauty.

"You mean NetCon, that IT multinational in sector five?" she asked slightly fazed, and I nodded.

"Wow! Some of my friends work there and they tell me that it hires the brightest minds in the industry," she said in a single breath, extending her hand too.

With that compliment, I was feeling proud of myself all of a sudden. You realize your worth only when a good looking girl praises you. With that smile that showed her halo white teeth, she looked just like a lit candle that drove all the darkness away.

"Yes, and you know what? We are all from the same college. And would you believe if I tell you that not only the same college, but also had the same ranks in the final year. All three of us stood second!" Raja added, springing on her. There was still no sign of guilt on the face of that uncouth person.

"Really! Same college, batch and ranks too! That's definitely a rare coincidence," she said, beaming but looking pleasantly surprised.

"Yes, but ranks will depend upon where you want to count from. Sarthak stood second from the top while Raja and I from the bottom!" said Ankur, smiling wide and taking a big casual bite from the cookie in his hand with a cracking sound.

Sarangi's laughter had no end while I looked at Ankur's shirt pocket where he had conveniently stuffed a few more cookies. Sarangi noticed that too. I was surely in the company of one dog, one pig and an angel.

"College topper and NetCon Consulting! That is impressive, glad to meet you!" she said politely, with that angelic smile. We were still shaking hands and her hands were softer than the Sleepwell pillow that I had bought two days back from a Shopper's Stop sale. I shook hands with her a few seconds more than I should have and she too realized that. With a parting smile, she turned towards Ankur to just say hello and then continued her chat with Raja. I was lucky to have got her maximum attention amongst the three of us.

"Guys, it was great catching up with you, but I need to rush now. My bosses will be mad at me as I am already late," she said, bidding goodbye to all of us and walking away, only to come back swiftly.

"Sorry, I forgot to ask you if Raja told you on how to avail a discount on any of the bakery items or coffee. All you need to do is to quote my name while placing the order. They will call me to verify and I will take care of it. Do you know you will be entitled to a whopping seventy-five percent discount? Fun na! Raja knows it all and can tell you more about it later," she said, looking at me.

"Sarangi, if a person who knows it all and yet his friends end up paying the entire bill, what would you like to call that person? I would call him a pig!" I said, looking at Raja with a grin. The sight of the cherubic Sarangi had made me forget the coffee episode and I was back to my witty self.

"Oh my god, Raja! Did you really do that? That's evil. Sarthak, forgive my absentminded friend Raja. You take my employee id – GV87007Kol. Quote it the next time you place an order here," she said, sounding disappointed at Raja, but trying to console me affectionately with her smile. Truth be told, her smile was infectious enough to leave a thousand men injured.

"Hey guys, I have to rush now! I will catch up with you some other day," she said waving at us and finally starting her evening shift. She had left the place but her fragrance was still in the air. Raja drove all of us back to our homes on his bike and there was an unusual silence. I was smiling, thinking about Sarangi, Raja was driving, and Ankur was munching on the cookies. That person who puts a smile on your face with just the thought of them, that smile is a secret between just you and her. I dropped Raja and Ankur at their homes and took his bike to my apartment in Starwood Estate.

"Sarthak, you look as happy as Larry these days? No work at office?" said the old watchman, opening the security gate with a wrinkled smile on his face.

"Nothing like that, Ramu Kaka. Just met someone to whom I feel connected," I said parking Raja's bike in the two wheeler parking. Ramu Kaka had been guarding the society for the last six years, but was known to be a rude guy. Rub of the matter was that Ramu Kaka had a family of five to support on a meagre salary of four thousand rupees. Despite being rude to others, he used to talk to me affectionately as I had given my old computer to his kids.

I unlocked the door of my apartment and the clock in front of me showed 11.00 p.m. It was time to hit the bed, but somehow I thought of checking my office emails. Listen to your intuition; it will tell you everything that you need to know. There was a mail from Rajan stating that he wanted to meet me urgently at eight in the office next morning. Rajan was a no-nonsense boss and after reading his email, it was surely sack time. I quickly switched off all the lights, hit the bed and tried sleeping, though in vain. Attempting to sleep after the radiant sight of Sarangi was not going to be easy. When reality is better than your dreams, then you are surely in love.

While Sarangi was all over my mind, I wanted to know a few things; first and foremost, how did Raja know her and why did he not tell us about her in college? She was a babe whose sight could stop a clock. All the four years in college, all he did was talk a whole lot of crap under the sun. May be she was Raja's girlfriend or, perhaps Raja had feelings for her. I did not even want to try my luck if that be the case. Even if Raja wasn't seeing her or wanted to see her, the possibility of her being single was by far remote. She was gorgeous, well-mannered and graceful, and anyone would fall for her. With Sarangi's thoughts running wild in my mind, the time had 1.00 a.m. Though I had a meeting early the next day, knowing Sarangi's relationship status was important too. I was clearly risking my meeting with Rajan in order to find out Sarangi's relationship status. It is amazing how far you can go when you have the right person in your mind.

I got up from bed and logged on to Facebook – a wonderful website that gives instantaneous information about anyone in the world. With the fast internet speed late in the night, Sarangi Sen's detailed profile page was in front of me in no time. In her profile picture, she was wearing a black low neck gown with her kohl-black hair plunging over her shoulders. Time seemed to have stopped. Facebook, however, is designed smartly in the sense that it doesn't reveal the relationship status of people who are not your friends. Mark Zuckerberg, the founder of Facebook, isn't my school or college buddy. So, I couldn't ask him to give me details about Sarangi's relationship status. Nonetheless, I had a buddy who could and it was none other than Raja himself. I looked at the watch and it was half past one. I had second thoughts about calling him at this hour, but as the wise say, the best time to act upon anything is *now*. I dialled Raja's cell number and predictably, the phone rang for quite a while before Raja picked up.

"At this hour? Is everything alright, dude?" said Raja in a heavy voice. A phone call at half past one can wake up a dead soul, let alone Raja.

"Dude, it is late so I will come to the point directly. How do you know this girl Sarangi, whom we met today in the hotel?" I asked.

There was a silence on the call for a minute or so. Raja was most likely wondering what I was up to well past midnight.

"Is that what you want to know at this hour?" said a knocked out Raja.

"Yaar, I know it is an odd time but how do you know Sarangi? If she is your girlfriend, drop the line, otherwise I need to know," I asked sharply again.

"Looks like someone has fallen in love at first sight! She lives in the same army complex as mine and her family is known to us for the last twenty years. Does that help soothe your restless nerves? Can I go back to sleep now please?!" he said almost pleading. Raja's answer however did not have the details needed to pacify the wild thoughts running in my mind.

"No, you can't, not before my last question. Is she going around with you or, anyone else?" I asked, probing further as the devil lies in the details.

"Nope. She is very much single now! Does that make you happy?" said Raja in a sleepy tone.

"Single now? What do you mean?" I asked, confused.

"She was going around with an army captain until six months back. Poor captain was killed in a terrorist ambush in Jammu. She was down for a long time but slowly she is getting around to forgetting Captain Vikram. But don't ever mention Vikram to her," said Raja, sounding serious for the first time in our conversation.

For a minute or so, I felt sorry and prayed for the deceased captain's soul, but Raja's other words about Sarangi being single were like an ice cube soothing a burn. Words have power, they begin and end wars, they create and destroy families, they break hearts and they heal them too.

"My friend, now that you know she is single, can I go to sleep now?" said Raja, sounding sleepy and wanting to hang up.

"Sorry brother to have called you at this hour. Please sleep like a log. This call could have waited until tomorrow," I said joyous, having known what I wanted to know.

"You know who you are? The biggest asshole in the world!" said Raja, before hanging up.

There was something in the air. I was euphoric to know that the girl who had mesmerized me was single. Someone has said it right, to someone you might be a line in the book and to someone you might be the book. I wanted to talk to her, tell her stories, make her laugh, and smile with her. My random fantasies with her continued till three in the morning. With Sarangi's thoughts in my head, the meeting with Rajan had evaded my mind. I had barely slept for a few hours when my phone buzzed. The law of karma had caught up. You can't sleep peacefully by screwing up other people's sleep by calling them past midnight. If you do that to them, then someone else will do it to you. This time the call was from my boss Rajan. I looked at the watch and it showed seven in the morning.

"If you were sleeping, I just thought I'd wake you up. You are seeing me at eight in the office, right?" said Rajan. Rajan was a forty something industry veteran, a workaholic and thorough professional. He had a great eye for attention to details and would give a tough time to anyone on the smallest of slips. I had seen lots of hard boiled people in my life but he was one that was done for around twenty minutes. People used to tell horror stories about him mercilessly throwing samosas at people in meetings in rage.

"Rajan, I couldn't sleep properly last night. Can we start our meeting half an hour late?" I asked politely.

"Smart fellow, if your coming in late was okay, why would I waste my time sending emails to you last night and now calling you in the morning! Do you think I am a joker in a Bombay circus?" said an exasperated Rajan, least bothered about my request. From the outset, the conversation had started on a wrong note.

"Sorry Rajan! I will be there sharp at eight," I said rendering an apology. Certain situations in life are non-negotiable and unfortunately with Rajan, every situation was like that.

"Try to be as quick as possible. If you can fly, all the more better!" said a livid Rajan, before hanging up. With Rajan's mood not good, it was time to rush to office. The day seemed to have started aligning along Murphy's Law: If you had a good time the previous evening, significant chances are that your next day will be screwed up. I quickly changed to office formals, ran downstairs and started my bike. I pulled the accelerator to the maximum and covered more than half the distance in the next ten minutes. I looked at the watch and it showed forty minutes past seven. At this speed, I could cover the remaining distance in the next ten minutes. Having feasted only on coffee and biscuits the previous night at The Grand Vilas, I was starving, and decided to stop by a roadside aloo poori shop. The plan was to finish my breakfast in ten minutes and use the remaining ten minutes to reach office. That was good maths; engineers are always good at it.

"Chhotu, get me one tea and one plate aloo poori, fast!" I said aloud parking my bike. Chhotu, a teenage boy employed at the shop, came out and started gazing at me.

"What are you looking at? Get me one plate aloo and two pooris, right now!" I reacted, seeing Chhotu staring at me and not paying attention to what I had said. I didn't want to be rude but there was no time to be polite.

"I am just wondering if two pooris will suffice for you? You look like you have been hungry for days!" said Chhotu. Even Chhotu was able to gauge my miserable state but not Rajan.

"Man! Then get me four pooris but be really quick!" I said, irritated. Chhotu ran inside the shop to get the aloo pooris. He had sensed the urgency. I looked at the watch and I still had fifteen minutes left for my meeting with Rajan. In no time, Chhotu came out running, holding a plate of aloo poori in one hand and a glass of hot tea in the other. Poverty makes adolescents immune to the atrocities of life, let alone the temperature of the tea. Before I could grab the first bite, my phone again started flashing Rajan's number.

"Trying to eat pooris here could just as well mean Rajan's samosas landing at my face in office. I definitely need to rush now. No, not rush but fly!" I said to myself remembering Rajan's words. There was surely some reason behind his frantic calls.

I poured some aloo sabji over the pooris and made a roll out of them. I stuffed two of them in my mouth and rolled the remaining two in a newspaper sheet and put them in the front pocket of my laptop bag. Leaving a fifty rupee note on the table, I ran towards the bike.

Chhotu smiled looking at my mixed up state. His humble job of serving people breakfast was better than mine at that point in time. I started the bike and raced it to the maximum. If your boss wants you to be in office at a particular time, somehow the distance to the office can't be covered in time precisely on that day. Racing full throttle, I managed to reach office at eight thirty, a mammoth thirty minutes late and now running a clear risk of facing a samosa splash.

"So what if Rajan throws samosas at me, I have poori rolls in my bag, which I can use if the need arises. Life is a two way street, guys!" I said, bracing myself.

As soon as I reached office, I parked my bike and entered the lift along with few other company folks. I was still catching up my breath when someone tapped at my shoulder.

"Congrats dude for this London assignment!" said someone from behind, but I couldn't recognize the voice. I couldn't turn around as the lift was jam packed. The lift reached the third floor and a few people moved out creating some space. I turned around and it was Diwan, the boss's golden boy. The specialty about Diwan was that he always had the inside news, owing to his constant flattering of the boss. He, however, was a loudmouth and in no time, the inside news would turn to Facebook gossip.

"London assignment! Now where was this coming from? I thought Rajan was mad at me the way he spoke to me in the morning!" I asked, confused.

"Mad or happy, that part I don't know, but he has got a new project in London that will run for two months. Client wanted the smartest guy in the team and Rajan wants you to handle it," said Diwan from somewhere at the back.

That news from Diwan left me eating my hat. Rajan's tone on the phone seemed as though he had seen me flirting with his wife.

"Two months in London and salary in pounds; it is a jackpot, my friend!" Diwan said.

Life is what happens to you when you are busy making other plans. Ever since the previous night, when Raja had confirmed Sarangi's single status, my joy knew no bounds. My mind was constantly devising innovative plans to meet or call her on some pretext and now this London surprise.

"When you already know that the boss wants me to travel, I am sure you also know the travel date?" I asked in a tizzy. The travel news had triggered a chain reaction of thoughts in my mind.

"All I can tell you is that you don't have much time in hand. Talk to the boss. He is just as desperate to talk to you!" said Diwan, smiling and going out towards the cafeteria.

I came out along with him but instead, went towards the office. I was already late and hence ran fast. No, I almost flew towards Rajan's chamber. As soon as I entered, I rammed into Rajan head on. That was a terrible start to the office day. Due to the head on collision, the newspaper roll that had aloo poori flew out of my bag and did a smooth landing on his shirt, making a Pablo Picasso oil painting on his neatly ironed white shirt. From the impact of the collision, the office files in his hand flew in all directions and he fell down on the floor with a thud. If that was not enough, in attempting to save him, my fist accidently hit him directly on the nose. Gosh, the day couldn't have gone more wrong. It appeared to the onlookers that I had punched him hard when I had no intention to do so. He was still lying on the floor rubbing his nose that had become red from my accidental but precise punch. For a moment, I felt like the great Mike Tyson having knocked the opponent out within minutes of the fight's start. I, however, kept a straight face. The team on the fourth floor ran towards the place of the collision.

"I am so sorry Rajan; did not see you in the rush!" I said, apologizing and extending one hand to offer him support to get up. With the other hand, I tried to wipe the aloo poori spill on the previously white but now stained Louis Philippe shirt. His nose was still red.

"See me in my room in five minutes!" Rajan said getting up from the floor, picking up his files and iPad. He briefly gazed at me before walking back to his chamber. His facial expressions were like 'thank you for the treatment darling but let us meet in my area'. By no means could I escape the samosa rain now. I walked gutted to my desk waiting for those cursed five minutes to be over.

A few minutes passed and I walked towards his cabin that had a transparent glass door. I tapped on the door, slightly opened it and asked politely if I could come in. The stain from the aloo poori spill was still shining brightly on his shirt. He was on a phone call with someone, with his staple breakfast lying on the table; a cup of hot tea with three samosas. He gestured for me to come inside and sit on the chair opposite to him. He was probably aiming to hit me point blank. I sat on the chair but placed my hands on the table to protect myself in the eventuality of a samosas being thrown at me.

"See, whatever I have told her has proven me right once again. She doesn't trust my knowledge but she definitely needs to," said Rajan ending his call and grinning.

It was good to see him mellowed down.

"Was it a new client? I hope we are getting some fresh business!" I asked, wanting to divert his attention from the punch incident.

"No, no! It wasn't a client's phone, but my wife's. Every Friday, we talk for thirty minutes to discuss important family matters. She makes the not-so-important decisions, while I call the shots for the most crucial ones, the ones that have maximum impact, you know what I mean?!" he said with a smile. The smile was a welcome indication that he had forgotten the collision fiasco.

"That's how a man should be, like a king!" I said, faking my interest in the husband-wife conversation when neither was it my business, nor did I have any experience in dealing with husband-wife matters.

"She decides what school the kids should go to or where we should go for our next holiday," said Rajan.

To me, family vacation or planning for kids' education were the most important family decisions than anything else. I wondered what decisions Rajan was making at home.

"My decisions have a global impact," he said, grinning and blowing his own trumpet.

"Global impact? Really?" I asked, surprised.

"Yes, I decide whether the United States should invade Iran or who should win in the forthcoming elections," he said, beaming and I smiled with him.

It was good to see his funny bone tickling minutes after the disaster. Now that he seemed to be in a better state of mind, I wanted to check the reason for his frantic calls in the morning as well as the news of my London posting that Diwan had broken to me.

"Rajan, you said in the morning that you wanted to meet me urgently," I said, reminding him.

"Oh yes! Thanks for reminding me. There is a new customer assignment that we have got in London," said Rajan on a high. "The news just came down to me last evening. They said that the workload is more, but they can only afford one consultant from us. They have also said that the person should be a smart guy. I am hoping that I can count on you," said Rajan, now almost requesting me.

For him, I was his horse for the course. Life at times gives you interesting choices. If I would have had said 'no', he would have been in a soup owing to his commitment to the customer. I must admit that I wasn't the brightest guy in Rajan's team, but I was surely the one to persevere and take all the tasks to their logical end. This trait of perseverance would later help me to play the dice with the invisible script of destiny. When I remember the traumatic time that came in my life, I wonder how I pulled it off, but when I look back in time now, the feeling is galactic. For now, let us stick to the conversation between me and Rajan.

"I know you will not let me down!" he said, still observing me thoughtfully and trying to convince me. Given his desperate calls in the morning, I had imagined this meeting to be a funeral and it was turning out to be a wedding. I kept mum while Rajan grew worried because of my silence. Between a glass half full and half empty, most people would think half empty, and so did Rajan. He assumed that I was reluctant to take up the offer.

"Doesn't London excite you? You will make good money in two months, plus the charm of the English weather," he said, trying desperately to convince me.

"If London is that good, why don't you go yourself? There are better people and things to do here, but how would you know about them!" I murmured, but kept that to myself. Better things included nothing else but the graceful and angelic Sarangi.

"What did you say?" asked a flabbergasted Rajan. He apparently heard a few words but not the entire statement.

"I said it will be amazing to go there, Rajan! It has been my dream to work in London," I said, smiling and nodding in affirmation. A smile is a curtain that will cover up a lot of your screw-ups.

"Excellent, my boy…! That's the spirit. That's the attitude. This is what makes you stand apart from the others! You will go far in life!" said a visibly euphoric Rajan.

I didn't know whether I would go far in life or not, but London was surely ten hours away. Even though I had little idea of the work that Waterloo Retail wanted, Rajan had faith in me. In life, all you need is ignorance and confidence, and success is sure to come.

"Here are your tickets and hotel booking that I did this morning," said Rajan, handing me printouts. The first print out was of my hotel booking in Reading, a small town in Berkshire, England. The second bunch of printouts were my travel tickets with Emirates Airways, with a stopover at Dubai and then from Dubai to London. While flipping through the pages, I noticed the travel time as 11:50 p.m., 30 March, 2014. There was something odd in this date and it didn't take me long to figure out that it was today's date. I looked at the watch and I had a meagre twelve hours in hand to get ready. It was time to rush back home to ensure my travel documents, clothes and other things that I would need in London were in place. While London would have helped me to earn some good money and every software engineer looks forward to that, two months was a long time to be away from Sarangi. We weren't even friends until now, but I had newfound fears too. What if she started liking someone else while I was away in London? This London assignment had come at twilight. A part of my mind wanted me to travel, but my heart said 'don't go'. I however had committed to Rajan and there was no looking back. As they say, life is a poop sandwich and every day you have to take another bite.

I came to my desk, switched off my computer and started driving back home. On my way back, the Science City traffic lights showed a red signal and I stopped. The traffic watch at

the signal showed hundred seconds remaining and it was time
to switch the engine off. Waiting for the signal to turn green, I
looked at the other side of the road and noticed one blue Scooty
rider wearing a helmet that had a dark glass cover, staring at
me. It could have been only a coincidence that the Scooty rider
and I looked at one another at the same moment. I did not pay
much heed to this trivial coincidence and started looking back
at the traffic signal. There was a lot going on in my mind as
I had to travel after a few hours to a different continent, and
barely fifteen minutes back, I had not even been aware of this
trip. I looked at the Scooty rider again and there was something
unusual about the way the Scooty rider was constantly gazing at
me. I was a little mixed up. Who could it be, staring at me like
this in a city where I was barely an year old? It couldn't have been
Raja or Ankur by the remotest possibilities, as they never wore
helmets. By now, the Scooty rider had started waving his hand at
me. I was gob-struck. I first looked at the Scooty rider, who was
still waving his hand and then at the traffic clock, which showed
twenty-two seconds to go. I wanted to gesture and ask who it
was. But wouldn't it for sure be insane to play dumb charades
on the busiest traffic signal in Kolkata? The only way to know
the identity of the driver and settle the curiosity in my mind
was to talk to the rider. Honestly speaking, with half a night's
sleep and so many things happening at the same time, my mind
had gone numb. Instead of pulling my bike on the roadside, I
parked it in the middle of the road, with at least fifty vehicles
in front of me and may be more than two hundred behind me.
I started walking towards the other side of the road where the
Scooty was. When hundreds of vehicles are behind you, parking
a vehicle like that was undoubtedly a senseless act. Whenever
a man does a thoroughly stupid act, it is always for the noblest
of motives. The traffic clock showed ten seconds still left for

the light to turn green. I ran fast, had reached the Scooty and managed to touch the rider's hand when the lights turned green. The touch of the rider's hand intuited me that I had known this person for ages. Who could that person be? With traffic lights turning green, a chunk of the traffic had started moving along with the Scooty. With the rider's face covered under the black helmet glass, despite being so close, I couldn't see who it was. It was also a bizarre act from the rider to wave at me for that long, but not stop when I was standing next to him. While I did not succeed in finding out who the Scooty rider was, I managed to click a photograph of the Scooty with my phone. WB 020H 6035 was the number and I saved it on the phone. In no time, one of the busiest traffic signals in Kolkata was deserted. Feeling hung up, I started walking back to my side of the road to pick my bike up, wondering about this bizarre incident. As they say, life is either horrible or miserable.

"*Eke dhoro!*" shouted someone from the back. I turned around and saw two agitated traffic sergeants running towards me.

"I am so sorry sir! I shouldn't have done this but..." I said, realizing my mistake of parking the bike in the middle of the road.

"But what mister?" questioned the tough looking cop, coming close and giving me black looks.

"Did you even bother to see how many vehicles were there? Your Spiderman-like stunts can risk so many lives!" said the less tough looking cop. I had indeed acted stupidly but stupidity isn't punishable by death. If it was, there would be a hell of a population drop.

"That blue Scooty rider was waving at me!" I said, confessing. Confession is a tonic for the soul when you have nothing else to say.

"Waving hand?! Is this Tollygunge club that you come to wave hands and meet people? Mister, this is the Science City signal that sees more than fifty thousand vehicles daily. And which blue Scooty? I can't see any Scooty around!" said the tough looking cop, hopping mad at my statements.

"The Scooty left when the lights turned green," I said slowly.

"Thank you for telling me that vehicles leave when the light turns green! You are not only a traffic rule offender but a smart liar too," said the tough looking cop.

"Trust me sir, whatever I am telling you is not a lie!" I said.

"Okay, for a moment I want to believe you. If that Scooty rider was known to you, why didn't it stop?" asked the cop looking at me suspiciously. His argument had weight.

"I have no idea why it did not stop!" I said. I indeed did not know myself why he hadn't stopped. At times, truth is stranger than fiction.

"Shut up! Stop telling me stories and show me your license!" said the tough looking cop. He was almost certain that I was trying to pull wool over his eyes.

"Yadav, let us do his breath test! I think he is drunk in broad daylight," said the tough looking cop to the other.

"I am not drunk, uncle! That rider indeed appeared familiar," I said, trying my best to convince him.

"Uncle? I am not your uncle! I am sub-inspector Prashanta Mukherjee who is known to put smart asses like you in the lock up!" said the tough cop, almost threatening me. The word 'lock up' sent shivers down my spine. It sounded too humiliating and untimely for an innocent software guy who was unwillingly headed towards London, but now looked all set to go to jail.

"I am so sorry sir! I promise I won't repeat it," I said, feeling repentant. I had messed up and the situation was out of hand.

With my head down, I managed to see that the tough looking cop had taken out a thick notebook from somewhere. I guessed he was going to fine me heavily.

"Come to Salt Lake police station after ten days, show this receipt and take your driving license back!" said the tough looking cop, tearing a receipt from his book and handing it to me, while keeping my license. I nodded obediently like a studious kid to wrap up the matter. License surrender and three hundred rupees was a trivial matter when compared to landing up behind bars. I put the receipt in my wallet and disappeared in no time and soon reached my flat.

It was the month of March and London at this time of the year was going to be cold. There was a shopping mall named Good Square close to my society and I shopped for necessary woollens, toiletries and other required things. I also bought a few packets of rice and lentils from there. With all the needed shopping done, I came back home, and slowly but steadily, managed to finish my packing in the next few hours. My watch showed six in the evening and that meant I still had two hours in hand to leave for the airport. In those two nervous hours, I checked my passport, air tickets and my hotel reservation at least twenty times and tried placing them in a, so to say, 'better and safe' place in my hand luggage. Truth be told, it was my first international trip and I was slightly nervous. Anxiety is like sitting in a rocking chair. It gives you something to do but doesn't get you anywhere.

The cab arranged by NetCon arrived shortly and took me to the departures gate of Netaji Subhash Chandra Bose International Airport. I timely completed the baggage X-ray, security check, immigration formalities and breathed. Owing to the collision melodrama in office with Rajan, I had missed out on lunch. So I bought a coffee and a cheese pizza while waiting for the boarding announcement. Soon after, boarding was announced and I, along with other passengers, boarded. The flight took off with a deafening sound and there was slight turbulence that subsided after some time. I plugged in my ear phones and listened to music. I did not even realise when I fell off to sleep. I was hardly asleep for an hour when I sensed a tap on my shoulder and it was an airhostess serving pizza slices, cookies and alcohol. Pizzas are good, but nothing can beat booze on an international flight. Sipping Johnnie Walker at an altitude of several thousand feet automatically gives you a different high. I requested the airhostess to bring me a few more glasses of Johnnie Walker as there is no such thing known as a small whisky.

My itinerary was Kolkata-Dubai-London and the plane landed at the Dubai International Airport. There was a stopover of two-and-a-half hours before my next flight to London. Dubai airport had a huge and sprawling air conditioned shopping area with countless luxury brands ranging from Mango, Levi's, Rolex, Nike and several others. Then there were duty free shops selling chocolates, electronic goods, clothing, perfumes, liquor, and greeting cards. The more you looked around, the more shops you'd see every time. With at least two hours in hand till my next journey from Dubai to London, I walked inside a greeting card store. I started flipping through cards randomly and it brought back the memories of college life. In our engineering college, Valentine's Day was celebrated with a lot of pomp and show. Boys in colleges can be safely categorized as two kinds: the first category is of street smart dudes who have regular girlfriends. The second category is of aspirants or hopefuls. Ankur, obviously, was the leader of the second category. Few days before Valentine's Day, he and I had gone to a card shop in the South-Ex market in Delhi.

"Can you show me some mushy Valentine's cards? Sentimental ones, you know what I mean?" Ankur said to the shopkeeper. The shopkeeper smiled, looked around in the shelves and took out one heart-shaped card.

"Here is the one for the lady love of your life! Look at the syrupy lines inside. She will fall in love the moment she opens the card," said the shopkeeper, showing it to Ankur.

"Then give me four of them!" said Ankur, and everyone in the shop laughed.

I suddenly realized that I was not in Delhi in South-Ex but at the Dubai airport and had already spent more than an hour at the shop. It was time to run for my second leg of the journey, from the country of Sheikhs to the country of the Queen. The plane took off with a roaring sound after a long run on the runway and was up in the air within a few minutes. I pulled up the window shutter and could see tiny buildings and cars moving on the road that slowly disappeared, and soon it was just the ocean and clouds beneath us. I slept for a while, drank a few more glasses of wine and shortly afterwards the plane landed at London's Heathrow Airport. I came out of the plane and completed all the immigration formalities. In no time, I was in front of a huge signboard that had 'Welcome to Heathrow London' written on it. There wasn't even a single desi person around me, but all well-dressed Englishmen. I looked up and thanked God for his kindness for fulfilling this dream of mine. Another sign board indicated the way to the taxi stand that was outside the airport. I wheeled my luggage outside of the airport and it was nature at its best. There were feather-like snowflakes falling from the sky, which had turned reddish black with a few swallows flying about. Doesn't snow have a way of softening things, of calming the rush of life and muffling the sounds? I stood there for a minute appreciating the radiance of nature. The only thing that could have been more mesmerizing and soothing than this would have been a glimpse of Sarangi. While I was miles away from her, she was in my mind all the time. Good times never last for more than a minute, and right then, it was broken by a high-pitched voice.

"Kidhar jaana hai?" asked a cab driver from inside a black cab, who appeared Asian from his looks, possibly a Pakistani or an Indian. I was pleasantly surprised at being welcomed in Hindi in the country of the Queen.

"Reading... Southampton Street," I said. It was the town where my guesthouse was located.

"Forty pounds!" he said and I nodded. Soon the cab was cruising through the highways of London, but nothing much was visible except street lights as it was dark. The cab soon reached the guesthouse. I checked in and slept for hours to nurse my jet lag. Over the next few days, I had started to adjust with the pace. My office hours were from nine till five and my English colleagues were ultra-polite who used 'please', 'may I', and 'thank you' excessively. It certainly felt good. After office hours, I regularly used to go to Sainsbury and the Tesco grocery stores. My breakfast included cereals with milk, lunch was sandwiches and dinner was self-made food – Maggi or a paneer roll if I had the luxury of time in hand. There was also a Hindu temple close to my guesthouse that used to arrange for free dinners every Tuesday for all in the vicinity. Obviously, it was a day that would run full house as free food has always and will continue to attract bachelors. We all have heard about the unpredictable English weather but I found it similar to that of a nice hill station in India, like Shimla or Darjeeling. In such weather, all you wish for is company of your friends and loved ones, and have boisterous fun all day. After office hours, the gloomy and dark evenings of London would depress me and I would miss Sarangi more, even though there was nothing between us.

Soon the rubber hit the road and work picked up impetus. I got busy with client meetings and working late hours. Rajan had said all good things about the project before my travel but had not uttered a word about the huge work load. I, however, did not create much of a fuss as it would have sounded unprofessional. It was better to light the candle than curse the darkness. Deeply buried in work, week after week passed by, and I did not get time to talk to Raja, Ankur or Sarangi. However, late in the night in my guesthouse room, the mere thought of Sarangi and her smirk used to bring a smile on my face. When you smile alone, you really mean it.

As the wise say, all good things (and bad things too) must come to an end. Amidst all the grinding work, eight weeks were over soon. The last day of the project finally arrived and I heaved a sigh of relief.

"Sarthak! You have done an excellent job for us in the last two months. I have noticed your emails coming into my inbox well past midnight and therefore I appreciate all the hard work. I will be calling Rajan to tell him about the professionalism that you have shown here!" said John Wong, my half-American, half-Chinese customer at Waterloo Retail.

I smiled, but my mind was in a different place. More than wondering what John would say to Rajan or how Rajan would congratulate me, I wanted to see Sarangi. Though we had spoken a little during the coffee meet, there was a magnetic feeling whenever I used to think of her. Love is elegant even when silent and distant. As they say, silence is the language of love, the rest is poor translation.

I came back to the hotel, paid my bills and got a cab to drop me to the airport. On my return stopover in Dubai, I bought two bottles of Chivas Regal whisky for the two dogs in India. I wanted to buy something unique for Sarangi as she had unintentionally carved out a special place in my heart. Finally, after contemplating a lot, I bought a Christian Dior perfume for her. I boarded the flight and it soon landed in Kolkata. I switched on my phone and dialled Raja's number.

"Guys, I am back! Where are you?" I said over on the phone, getting excited. "I have got bottles of Chivas Regal scotch whisky. It will go down like nectar this evening."

"Awesome my friend, awesome! You are indeed an intelligent guy," said an ecstatic Raja.

"Intelligent? Now, where is this 'intelligence' thing coming?!" I asked, surprised by the untimely appreciation.

"These aren't my words, my friend. This is what Sarangi tells me about you every time she calls me," said Raja.

"Really?" I asked, pleasantly surprised.

"Yes, anyway Ankur and I are coming to your home right away. We will get fish tandoori packed on the way from Shiraz Golden restaurant," said a grinning Raja. "By the way, what else did you buy from London?"

"Nothing much. A Christian Dior perfume!" I said after pausing.

"Ahem... ahem!" said Raja, trying to artificially clear his throat and I could sense a smirk on his face. It was a no brainer for him to guess for whom the perfume was. I missed my friends, our addas and Ankur's amusing poor jokes and crappy language. But most of all, I had missed Sarangi in the two months that had seemed like two decades. I wanted to find out if she had missed me too. A man has a choice to begin love, but not to end it.

Love Blossoms but
Blushes too

⌘

"May I come in"? I asked, tapping on Rajan's cabin's glass door.

"Come in, my champion! Look here, John just sent me a big email about your fantastic work in London. He is so pleased with your work that he wants to give us two more projects. Good show my boy, good show!" said a visibly charged up Rajan.

"And dude, you almost got me killed with the work!" I murmured in a low volume, keeping it to myself.

"Sorry, did you say something?" asked Rajan, a little confused. He had apparently heard a few words, but not the entire statement.

"I said you bet on the right horse, boss! It was a tough project, but I managed!" I said.

"Yes, that is why I had sent you. I have this knack of spotting the right talent and that is why I am a vice president at forty!" said an ecstatic Rajan, blowing his own trumpet. "But you know what? I have failed in certain areas too."

"You and failed! Where? How?" I asked a little surprised. Rajan was extremely street smart and it was difficult to believe him failing at something.

"Even after fifteen years of my marriage, one thing which I am still trying to understand is what women want!" he said, as happy as a Larry and I smiled with him too.

Though Rajan was my manager, he was becoming more friendly with me after this London assignment. A winning man is never short of friends, after all.

"Let us talk about the project," he said, changing the topic just when I thought he would be at peace after I had completed the project. What the heck! I had returned only a day before after such an intense project, and he wanted to talk about it even after it was over. Some men are animals and can be shot for food or fur!

"John told me about how hard you worked, sometimes on weekends too. He has promised to give us two more projects, but only if you are in the team," said Rajan on a high.

"Do I need to travel again?" I asked, taken aback. I definitely did not want to work this hard and stay away from my loved ones to make money. If working like a donkey was the only way to prosper in life, then donkeys would have been richer than Bill Gates.

"No, this project will be worked upon in India, but in UK timings. Hope that is okay with you," he said, grinning.

I sighed with relief and came out of his cabin. I was jetlagged but still did not want to go home. I instead wanted to go to The Grand Vilas to see the loveable beauty, Sarangi. I had kept that Christian Dior perfume in my bike but wasn't confident about giving it to her. Maybe she liked me or maybe she didn't, but no one had said anything to one another for fear of rejection and getting hurt.

I came down to the parking lot, and before I could start my bike, my phone rang and it was Rajan again on the line.

"Before you leave office, can you please fill your time sheet?" said Rajan, and it sounded more like an order than a request.

"Will Pakistan attack if the timesheet is filled tomorrow?" I said to myself, making a song and dance about it. Parking the bike, I unwillingly came back to my desk and starting filling the time sheet when my phone rang again.

"Now what else do I need to do?" I said to myself without looking at the phone, assuming it to be Rajan again.

"Seema from reception!" said Seema, the not-much-to-look-at receptionist of NetCon who purposefully wore skimpy clothes to attract young campus recruits in the office.

"There is a visitor for you at the reception! Do you want to come down?" she said on the line.

"It must be that asshole credit card guy! I had told that pushy good for nothing fellow to come after a week, but who listens to me these days!" I said, making a fuss. I was irritated as my plan to go and see Sarangi was derailed.

"Will you please mind your language?" she said, amused upon hearing the crappy words in my language. "Come down soon. The visitor doesn't seem to be from a credit card company. I have other calls to take. Bye!" she said, apparently smirking.

The day was hit by Murphy's law from all corners. First Rajan had wrecked my plan to go to The Grand Vilas, and now presumably this credit card person had come to collect his payments. All things go wrong at once. I went to the ground floor reception but couldn't find anyone other than Seema wearing a low neck top, busy connecting the phone lines. While on the phone, she gestured that my visitor had stepped out. Fair enough! Life is not as good as you think, but it is not as bad either. I came out of the office building and looked around, but still couldn't see anyone. That was strange! I walked towards the visitors parking area at the back of office and could see only three vehicles parked; a Hero Honda bike, an old white Santro and one blue Scooty. The first two vehicles looked like they had been parked there for ages with multiple coatings of dust on them. If at all my visitor had a vehicle, it would have been that blue coloured Scooty. There was something about that Scooty. I looked at it for more than a minute and it occurred to me that I had seen this number somewhere before. It didn't take me long to figure out that it was the same Scooty for which I had created a melee at the Science City traffic light and had invited the wrath of traffic cops a couple of months back. The mystery on the driver's identity, however, was still unresolved.

"Hi, Sarthak!" came a chirpy and a euphonious voice from somewhere behind me. I turned around and it was none other than the gorgeous Sarangi looking at me with her constellation-blue eyes and a beam on her face. The best feeling in the world is when you are looking at that special person and he or she is already smiling at you. Wearing a red top and a pair of low waist black jeans, she was looking beautiful. Her sight had abated all the cusses running in my mind, my jet lag and the timesheet. It was a weird day as I had met with two extreme people in the last ten minutes; one who wanted me to fill the timesheet before leaving for The Grand Vilas and the other one was the gorgeous beauty, for whom I could kill a thousand men.

"Good to see you after this long!" said Sarangi. She extended her hand to shake mine and I pinched my forearm to ensure that this wasn't a dream arising from the jetlag.

"Good to see you as well, Sarangi!" I said, wanting to hug her, but controlled myself to only shaking hands with her.

Although I shook it longer than I should have. She smiled. Every time you smile at someone, it is an act of love and a gift to that person.

"Two months seemed like a decade to me. Raja told me that you were back from London and I thought I would come to see you," she said, chirping, but I could sense a few lines of worry on her forehead. She was clearly disturbed by something.

"Is everything alright, Sarangi?" I asked, seeing her disconcerted.

"No, nothing…I haven't discussed it with anyone but thought I will talk to you once you are back," she said.

"Tell me what is bothering you?" I asked, concerned.

"There is some politics going on in my office and I am unwillingly caught in it. I wanted to talk to you to understand how to handle this rumpus," she said, sounding apprehensive. From being chirpy minutes ago, her face had shades of sadness.

"Who is troubling you? I am very good at shooting at people's bums with my dad's licensed revolver!" I said and she seemed better, displaying that halo white smile. I noticed that her lips were puffy and definitely kiss-inspiring.

"Hey, before that, on the other day it was you at the traffic signal, right?" I said and her face that could stop a clock lit up.

"You know what? I was shouting aloud and wondering why you weren't able to hear me but realized later that my helmet glass cover was on. How stupid I am! And by the time you reached my Scooty, the traffic light had turned green," she said with her clear blue, but apologetic eyes.

"Wow, how convenient! And the traffic cops had my ass!" I said smiling. She giggled hearing my crappy language and I noticed that we were still shaking hands.

"Sorry about my language! I picked that from some asshole guys in college," I said, without realizing that I was still cussing.

"Oops!" I uttered and she couldn't control her laughter.

"The most trustworthy person who can help me dealing through this merry hell, I think, is you," she said with starry eyes that were filled with hope.

I did not know how she had this perception that I could handle politics. In fact, I hated politics. Politics is designed to make lies sound truthful and murder respectable. Nonetheless, I understood on that day that somewhere she had started to trust me even though we had met just once. There are times in life when being trusted is a greater compliment than being loved.

"I am so sorry! I didn't realize that you have just arrived from a long journey and I started my universe of cribbing. You please go home, get some rest and I will meet you some other day," she said, sounding apologetic realizing that I was silent and in deep thought.

I was indeed thoughtful but was actually thanking Rajan, who had told me to be in office to fill the timesheet; else Sarangi and I would have never crossed paths and wouldn't have met. Was it a coincidence? As they say, don't dismiss coincidences; they are signals. You will relate to this saying better when these coincidences will appear at different times helping me to take on the biggest challenges in my life or anyone's life if you will. For now, let us stick to the banter that was going between us.

"Hey, no! Sorry I was thinking about something else. Shall we go to your hotel and catch up over coffee one more time? With you around, I am sure there will be no screw up on the discount!" I said, grinning, and upon hearing this, there was an instant gleam on Sarangi's face and spark in her doe-like eyes.

"How about coffee at the Café Coffee Day in City Center-I? In the hotel, the staff will be hovering around us all the time!" she said subtly. I noticed that she was sensitive about small things while I had a care-a-damn attitude in life.

"And since I am troubling you, coffee is on me!" she said sweetly.

"Well, being friends means no conditions put and never having to say sorry," I said, smiling, and she beamed.

Saurabh Talukdar, another cheesy guy in my team, was returning from a *sutta* (cigarette) break and noticed me talking to Sarangi in the visitor's parking lot. After having looked at us laughing together, he seemed frustrated. Sarangi's radiance could injure a thousand married men, let alone mean souls in office.

"I thought the boss wanted you to fill a timesheet!" said a jealous looking Saurabh.

"Whether my timesheet is filled or not is none of your business, but does your father know you smoke?" I spat back.

Both of us used to share a common desk phone and Saurabh's parents used to call him a lot. If I would have told them about his chain smoking, he would have had a tough time at home. Saurabh was taken aback.

"Boss, never ever utter these words to them. No one has ever smoked in three generations of my family and I will be thrown out of the house if any one comes to know of this," said a terrified Saurabh, realizing that he had picked the wrong battle.

"Then you better mind your own business. You have a lot of tasks to finish!" I said, reacting sharply.

I wasn't a guy who's into bullying, but one shouldn't let people take one for a ride. Seeing me charged up, he vanished into thin air in no time. I looked at Sarangi and she had admiration on her face and a strange confidence. In my unintended wooing of her, she looked up, fluttered her eyelids and said, "You argue well."

It appeared to me that this conversational brutality had taken her breath away. Her facial expression indicated that I was exactly what she secretly longed for – a man who could save his woman by standing up fearlessly against the world.

"Okay then. We will go to Café Coffee Day in City Center I. You follow my bike on your Scooty," I said.

City Center I is one of the big open air malls in Kolkata that has a spacious Café Coffee Day. I wanted us to go on one bike but at the same time, I did not want to sound desperate.

"Won't one bike be good? I have always wanted to enjoy the speed of a motorcycle, but never got a chance. My father has a Bullet 500cc, but doesn't let me touch it. He says I will end up breaking my bones with it and that I am fit only for a scooty. Never mind, let us go on our own bikes. You drive in front and I will follow you on my Scooty. Okay?" she said, wearing her helmet and starting her Scooty.

Life is a bitch. Things that one desires in life are achieved by being courageous and I had screwed a golden opportunity. If now I would have suggested going on my bike, I would have looked like an idiot. She had already started her Scooty and now there was no point in crying over spilt milk. We were soon on our way to City Center I.

"A table for two," I said to the waiter who received us at the entrance and quickly guided us to a table next to a window that had a good view.

"Beautiful lady first," I said pulling a chair for Sarangi. She was looking as zinger as ever. We were constantly gazed at by a bunch of guys, including some familiar faces from NetCon. By now, it was almost certain that 'Sarthak dated a babe' would be the news tomorrow at NetCon.

She started describing the office politics that was bothering her. She had two reporting managers and was getting caught between their ego clashes. A typical case of pulling wires. I understood that the second manager would tell her to do the opposite of what the first had requested, leaving her at sixes and sevens and unable to carry out any of her work in the hotel.

"Do both of them have the same boss or different bosses?" I asked, trying to understand the details as the devil lies in detail.

"Same boss, the general manager of the hotel," she said with a concern in her voice.

"Got it! Drop a mail to the general manager requesting for a meeting. Tell him that you have some ideas that will help improve hotel performance," I said. I had worked out a plan according to the way I would have handled it. I have been called arrogant at times, but arrogance sometimes translates to having the guts to take on some big challenges in life. We will be there shortly. Stick with me.

"Improving the hotel's performance? But the problem is me handling these two guys and not the hotel's performance!" she said, looking astounded.

"See, improving the hotel performance is the carrot for the general manager, so that he gives you time. If you send an email to him about what is bothering you, he won't be interested, trust me," I said, starting to unveil the plan.

"I am confused. I can't follow that," she said, looking very confused. With every question she was asking, I was falling in love with her. Someone has said it right, all first love letters are written with the eyes.

"Long time back, I had a smart Catholic friend, who used to religiously visit the church every Friday, but he was a chain smoker. He once asked the priest if he could smoke while he was praying and the priest went ballistic on him. Of course, you can't smoke while you are praying, right?" I said.

"Yes, you shouldn't smoke while praying but what has that got to do with these two guys and my office politics?" she asked, fazed.

"After a few days, when the priest had forgotten the incident, my friend went again and asked if he could pray while he was smoking. Priest said yes, any time for prayer was fine!" I said grinning, and she appeared lit up. A smile is the light in your window that tells others that there is a caring and sharing person inside.

"Once he agrees to have a meeting, tell him how both of these assholes have been giving you overlapping tasks to perform and how it is impacting hotel's efficiency. Also tell your general manager that these two guys should coordinate between themselves before assigning any task to you," I said with a chuckle.

There was a silence for a minute followed by a big beam on her face.

"Oh my god, that is amazing. This is how you mesmerize people around you. See, I knew deep down within that if I talk to you, all of my problems would be sorted," she said, holding my hand in enthusiasm.

Some people touch your hand and reach your heart, and it was a touch like that. We were bonding well. I gave her a few more suggestions, some amusing, some serious and we laughed every time. Her halo white teeth reminded me that the toothpaste in my house was finished. Amidst our chatting, we finished our coffee too. Filling up a timesheet in office for ten minutes seemed like ten hours, while sitting with the gorgeous Sarangi for one hour seemed like a minute. Rarely in life there comes a time when everything seems to be going right, and we call that time magical. This time was like that. I paid the bill and we came down to pick up our bikes.

"Accha listen, I have added you on WhatsApp. I will send you all sorts of funny messages!" she said, beaming, only to start her Scooty and bid me goodbye. I realized that I was continuing to wave my hand at her even after she had disappeared from sight.

I rode back home, threw my laptop bag on the sofa and decided to hit the bed. With Sarangi's thoughts running in my mind, sleep wasn't coming anywhere close to me. Finally at four in the morning, I managed to get some sleep. I had hardly slept for a few hours when the newspaper boy rang the bell. I looked at my watch and it was seven in the morning. With just three hours of sleep, it was going to be a difficult day ahead. As they say, if the previous day was spent well, there are high chances that the next day will be screwed up. I reached office at nine and the day looked loaded with fifteen e-mails from John Wong, my customer. With this huge workload piled up, I got coffee for myself to give my mind an illusion that it was awake. By lunch time, I had finished four cups of coffee and my mind was running as if it was being pulled by ten horses. With almost all the work done by the afternoon, I thought of taking a break and opened Facebook on my computer. Before the page could load properly, there was a WhatsApp notification on my phone. I opened it and it was from the celestial beauty Sarangi.

"What's up? How is the day so far?"

"Good. Facebooking. How are you?" I WhatsApped back.

"Wow, what fun. No work kya?" she said with four smileys.

"All work and no play makes me a dull boy!" I replied.

"C'mon, you are not dull, but a super intelligent friend of mine. After talking to you, I spoke to the general manager and he has given both the managers a good piece of his mind. Both of them seem quite scared now. I'm sorted out and much at peace," she responded, with another smiley.

"I am a consultant. My consulting gyan is not for free," I jested.

"Lunch at Peter Cat, Park Street...?" she asked. Our banter was picking up well. Before I could say anything, there was another message.

"Add me on Facebook. I have sent you a request just now."

If everything seems to be going well, you have obviously overlooked something. I saw Mr. Workaholic, I mean Rajan, coming towards my desk.

"Boss is around, will ping you back," I replied, put the phone in my pocket and closed the Facebook window.

I started gazing at the desktop screen as if I was solving a problem that had endangered the human race. Rajan just glanced at my desktop.

"Keep up the hard work, my boy!" said Rajan, tapping my back and continued his walk.

"Yes boss," I said, pretending to be deeply engrossed in solving a problem that never existed.

"I am back," I WhatsApped back.

There was no response from her. Her 'last seen at' status was two minutes ago. She seemed to have got busy with her work. Life is a bitch!

I too started focusing on my Java program and managed to finish it by evening. I checked WhatsApp again but her 'last seen at' was still at two in the afternoon. Her last WhatsApp message had said 'Add me on Facebook. I have sent you a friend request'.

On my way back home, I got chicken biryani parcelled from Shiraz Golden restaurant at E.M. Bypass that is well-known for its Mughlai food. I opened the door of my apartment and kept the biryani parcel on the table. The delightful dinner could wait as there were more important things to take care of – Sarangi's Facebook request. I accepted her friend request. I started going through her profile and she looked easy on the eye in all her snaps. I understood from her profile that she was a foodie, loved cakes and pastries, and her favorite perfume was Christian Dior, which coincidentally was the same brand that I had got for her from London but was still lying with me. Every event in your life is a dot and it will get connected somehow if your intention is good. I spent the entire night looking at her posts and photographs. I looked at my watch and it showed six in the morning. It was going to be a second consecutive work day without sleep, and stimulants like coffee don't work beyond a certain point. Luckily it was a Friday and for Englishmen like John Wong, Friday is as good as a weekend. The work load was less, so I finished it comfortably, came back home and slept like a log. I got up at eleven the next day and felt sane. It was a Saturday and the next day was Sunday, 3rd June, when I had blessed the mother earth with my arrival. Happy birthday to a person who is smart, good looking and funny.

Raja, Ankur and I connected over phone and decided it was to be Blue Express in Sector Five, Salt Lake for the celebration. It was a weekend, the time was decided and invitees too. Game on!

Soon all of us were at Blue Express in the afternoon. I was in two minds whether to invite Sarangi; a part of my mind wanted to invite Sarangi and a part said 'slow and steady wins the race'.

"There is a booking for three people under my name, 'Sarthak Arora'," I said to the lady at the reception.

"Yes, I have a table for four, but you are three. I hope that will be okay?" the lady said, showing us the table that was reserved for us. The restaurant was crowded but we were good as long as we had a place to wine and dine.

"Happy birthday, dude! May your birthday come twice every year," both of them said aloud in the same vein and soon the whole crowd in the restaurant sang 'happy birthday' for me. I felt loved and honoured.

"On this birthday of our friend, we have pledged to finish the entirety of alcohol from earth to save future generations. Get us six bottles of beer to start with and we will order more!" Raja said to a waiter. We raised a toast together to our magical friendship, that was beyond boundaries.

"Three plates of chana bhatura, two full roasted chickens, two plates of black dal, and ten tandoori rotis! Before that, get us three plates of chat and one plate of puchka. These guys will not eat the puchkas but I love them. Make them as spicy as possible. Once we have finished all this, please get us three kulfis!" Ankur ordered in a single breath like a Second World War refugee who had not seen food for years.

"Slow down, sir! You are a Formula One car and I am a bullock cart," said the waiter, trying to catch up with Ankur's speed.

"Guys, I skipped last night's dinner and this morning's breakfast as well to make the most of today's lunch!" said a philosophical sounding Ankur, taking a sip of beer. Alcohol is a magical drink that turns normal human beings into a 'seen it all, been there, wise' philosophers.

"Dude, is this the only list of food that you want to order? You can still add to your order if you think we have missed something?" I said, pulling Ankur's leg.

"I don't know if Ankur has missed anything, but I can tell that Sarthak is missing someone for sure and I think that someone is missing Sarthak too. Shouldn't she also be here?" asked Raja with a smirk on his face.

Best friends know what one does not even say. I was indeed missing Sarangi, but I did not want to seem desperate by inviting her. It could be out of line and could end up hurting myself by losing this beautifully carving relationship.

"I see! Our techie pal not only works smart but also has a love life! Looks like Raja also knows about it and the only asshole who has no clue of what is cooking is me," said a flabbergasted Ankur.

"Marwari, you need to take time out of your family's money minting business to be aware of the juicy gossip in town," said Raja smirking. "It is the same girl, Sarangi Sen, whom we met in the hotel."

"That hot babe, sorry I mean bhabhiji, is now Sarthak's girlfriend?! I see," said Ankur with eyes twinkling in surprise.

"Boss, let me clarify there is no girlfriend-boyfriend stuff here, hardly a friend. She wanted my opinion on something, and that's all. We aren't dating or hanging out, for your information," I tried trivializing the matter. We were friends, it wasn't yet love between us, but there was surely something that felt good. Was it love? No one knew.

"Dude, let me add some colour here. The way she loves to talk non-stop about you, anyone can make out she has a crush on you!" said Raja, spilling the beans. I was pleasantly surprised. You feel your worth only when a good looking girl praises you.

"Do you want to call her here? You've known her for a long time. I think she would come if you call her," I said, looking at Raja, whose facial expression indicated that he would rather want me to dial Sarangi.

Seeing my face light up in hope, Raja dialled Sarangi's number. I could hear Sarangi's voice from Raja's old phone that worked only in speaker mode.

"Thank you for the invite Raja, but I won't be able to make it today! The duty manager from last night did not turn up and I ended up doing his shift too. You see, it has been sixteen hours non-stop that I have been working. I just want to hit the sack now. Please don't feel bad but I don't think I can make it to the lunch!" she said, politely turning down Raja's invitation.

Knowing that she wouldn't be coming, I felt a little low. I looked at Raja and Ankur, and both of them felt gutted too. They were my buddies and cared for me. Soon, the food arrived.

"If not Sarangi, at least the food has arrived!" said Ankur, breaking the ice and picking up a big piece of chicken.

"Dude, what's wrong with you? Why don't you give her a call? If worse comes to worst, she won't come, and she isn't anyway," said Raja, taking the last sip of his beer.

Raja was trying to cheer me up but he was Sarangi's childhood friend. When Sarangi turned down Raja's invitation, I assumed the chances of her saying yes to my invitation were almost nil. And that is precisely where most of us go wrong. Assumptions more often than not, make an ass of us.

I was still confused. I did not want to disturb her after her marathon sixteen-hour shift, but wanted her to be here with me as well. Still at the sea, I dialled her number.

"Hi! What's up?" she said sounding sleepy, but as sweet as nectar.

"I think Raja had called you a few minutes back. What he didn't tell you is that it is my birthday today and I was wondering if you could come over. Raja, Ankur and I are already here!" I could hardly complete my statement when she interjected.

"Oh my God! Why didn't you tell me earlier? Looks like you still don't consider me your friend? Where are you now?" she asked, sounding energetic all of a sudden.

"Blue Express, Sector V! But before that, Raja was saying that you just finished a sixteen-hour shift. Wouldn't it be tiring for you to come?" I asked.

"For such a wonderful occasion, I could go anywhere, any time. Yes, Raja did call me a minute back, but he did not tell me that you three were together and that it was your birthday. Absent minded guy! He has always been like that ever since I have known him," she said chiding Raja, but I could sense an excitement in her voice.

"And shouldn't the birthday boy, my intelligent friend, invite me himself?" she asked.

Raja and Ankur with their mouth full of food were trying to gauge our conversation. Now that she was excited to come, I wanted to invite her in a special way which wasn't possible in front of dogs. For the words that need to come from your soul, you need solitude.

"Can I have the pleasure of having the beautiful lady here? Her company will be cherished," I said on the phone at a distance from our table.

"Now that's like my buddy! Give me twenty minutes, I will wear my new dress," she said.

"Just come as you are. I stop breathing when I look at you either way!" I said. My words could have been ahead of time, but it was better to have loved and lost than never loved at all.

"See you in ten minutes then!" she said in her songbird sweet voice. One word frees us from the pains and weight of life, and that word is 'love'.

I came inside and looked at Raja and Ankur. They were busy tucking into the pani poori, chana bhatura and butter chicken at the same time. Sarangi had said ten minutes but dispersing the next ten minutes appeared like a decade in a lonesome desert. I learnt a new thing on that day: a girl's 'I will be there in ten minutes' and an IT guy's 'I will be in office in ten minutes' are actually the same thing. I looked at my watch; twenty more minutes had passed and still there was no sign of her.

"Dude, she is the daughter of an army lieutenant. If she has given her word, she will surely turn up!" uttered Raja slowly, mixing up words as he had his mouth full.

"Waiter, get me a tooti fruity ice-cream!" said Ankur, and I was rather shocked at yet another order. The reason behind the world's food shortage wasn't famine and wars, but these two guys.

Amidst the madhouse, I suddenly felt Sarangi was somewhere close by. Listen to your intuition. It will tell you everything you need to know. I saw the restaurant door open and the vivacious Sarangi stepped in. Dressed up in a green sleeve-less top that had a low neckline and white slim fit jeans, she looked as they say, 'a picture'. She, with that innocent smile, waved at me from the door and I waved back joyously. When your joy comes from other people's smile and your smiles come from other people's joy, you are in love. She was holding a big gift wrapped packet in her hand. I looked at the dogs, Raja and Ankur, and they could only wave their hands at Sarangi as their mouths were loaded with chana bhatura and Pepsi.

"Wishing a very happy birthday to my dear friend Sarthak!" she said, walking towards me and giving me a soul-enriching hug that lasted for more than a few seconds.

Love those people who like you, hug you, who put their arms around you when you're not so lovable. With Sarangi walking in, the restaurant that had a dark ambience appeared lit up. While Raja and Ankur were busy eating, she carefully placed that gift-wrapped packet on the table and diligently unwrapped it. It was a big round black forest cake that had 'Happy birthday to my complete friend, Sarthak' written on it. She placed an 'S' shaped candle on the cake and lit it up, a gesture that touched me deep, as 'Sarthak' means complete. With every passing moment, I was falling in love with a girl that I hardly knew. Love is life. And if you miss love, you miss life.

"Can you take a snap for us please?" said a bubbly Sarangi, handing over her Samsung Galaxy phone to the waiter. "Say cheese guys!"

"Happy Birthday dear birthday boy! Birthdays are nature's way of telling us to eat more cake," she said putting a big slice in my mouth after I had cut the cake and the shutterbug clicked instantaneously.

Raja and Ankur both nodded in appreciation on Sarangi's public display of affection towards me. It was indeed heart touching. She took a small helping of the food while Ankur and Raja turned their focus towards the cake after having finished the chana bhatura, nans, butter chicken, lassi, Pepsi and ice-cream. We all were having a whale of a time when it occurred to me that though Sarangi was participative, she appeared fatigued. It was possibly owing to her sixteen-hour shift.

"Are you fine Sarangi? I know we are having a bash, but you haven't slept for almost twenty hours," I said, as I was concerned and had started caring for her.

"Oh, I am fine. I just have a slight headache, but it is manageable," she said

"Guys, Sarangi is not well and I am going to drop her home!" I said, and both of them nodded as Sarangi looked visibly fatigued. I paid the bill and we all came out of the restaurant. Before getting on his bike, Ankur walked close to me and whispered, "Dude, bhabhiji is hot, and you have got to control yourself. You have got to look in front and not at the pillion seat."

"Asshole," I said, giving Ankur angry looks. Both of them soon vanished on their smoke-oozing 500cc Yamaha. I also started Sarangi's Scooty and she sat pillion, encircling me with her arm. While driving, her hair would fly by my face and I could feel her nose nuzzling my back at times.

"Are you feeling any better? We should be at your place soon. Just lock your room and sleep like a baby," I said, racing up the Scooty.

"Oh, much better! Shall we drive till the airport, come back and then you drop me? The weather is so good," she said with effervescence back in her voice. She seemed to be enjoying the ride as the airport was another ten kilometres away while her house was just around the corner.

"Do you want to get admitted to a hospital tomorrow? No ride business. You should simply go and sleep!" I said, instructing her as if I had known her for years. Truth be told, I had starting caring for her. I stopped the Scooty as we neared her house.

"Birthday boy, it was a superb celebration. I loved every bit of it there. But you know what, the Scooty ride was the best part," she said, getting down.

"You just go, sleep and get up only when the next day is up. That is what I do every Friday!" I said, smiling.

"Not now, but only after I upload the birthday photographs on Facebook," she said with a sweet smile on her face.

"WhatsApp me once you reach home!" Sarangi said, giving me a short hug and starting her Scooty. The sky had turned reddish black and it had started to drizzle, while she drove her Scooty towards her house. About to disappear inside the gate, she took a u-turn and started coming back. I gazed at her while raindrops continued to fall. Stopping her vehicle at a little distance, she walked towards me. She had come so close that I could sense her breath and smell the rain droplets on her face. Looking at me with her constellation blue eyes, she pecked on my left cheek. I had always thought we were just good friends, but I was wrong. I put my hands around her twine sculpted waist and this time we kissed for long. It felt magical. The rain had started to pour heavily by now. Blushing, she started her Scooty and rode towards her home, this time to disappear inside. I stood in the rain, letting what just happened sink in. It doesn't have to be on Valentine's Day or New Year's Eve. It doesn't have to be by the time you turn eighteen or thirty-five. It just has to be; in time, in place, in spirit. It just has to be.

A Visit to Starwood Estate

⌘

An early morning Facebook notification woke me up. I glanced with my sleepy eyes and saw the birthday celebration snaps, including the one where she was putting a piece of cake into my mouth. These snaps had been uploaded at eleven in the night and by seven in the morning, there was a 'like' riot. The snaps had got a whopping one hundred and five 'likes' and fifty-two comments. My eyes got wide open and sleep seemed to have vanished. I tried looking at the first comment and it said:

"OMG, your boyfriend is soo cute! Where did you find him?"

Man, I was already labelled as her boyfriend. Good and bad, both. I quickly scrolled down and the last comment was from Diwan, the office news messenger.

"Two of you look good dude. Have a happy life ahead"

I reached office around nine and every face seemed to be smiling at me, including Rajan's. I smiled back at them, of course, a fake one. This Facebook post remained the hot topic of discussion in office for the next one week.

A few days later, Sarangi and I were talking over phone while I was in office when she made a strange request.

"I am coming to your apartment this Sunday!" The hot tea cup in my hand almost slipped hearing this.

I have never understood why girls always want to visit bachelor boys' rooms? What do they try to analyze there?

"My apartment... But why?" I asked.

"You don't want me to?" she asked. I could sense an immediate disappointment in her voice and could imagine her galaxy blue eyes turning sad.

"No, it is not that I don't want you to come. The rub is that my landlord is strictly against any booze or any of my friends visiting my apartment, let alone girls. Even when Raja and Ankur come, I tell him a day in advance." I tried to reason.

"If you give a day's notice for Raja and Ankur, you can give two days' notice for me. No?" she said, chuckling.

"Do you want me to be thrown out of the society?" I said jesting.

"I don't know. You deal with people around the world giving them smart sales talk. Shouldn't handling your landlord and letting me into your apartment be a cake walk for you? If you don't want me to come, then it is a different thing," she said, getting sentimental.

She wanted to come and I had to somehow manage that. Simply put, there was no escape route.

"Okay baba, you come on Sunday. I will take care of Mr. Roy," I said with conviction, even though I didn't even have the slightest idea how I would manage it. Of course, I couldn't have afforded to disappoint her. An ox is known by its horns and a man by his words.

"That is now my buddy talking! Today is Friday and I will be in your apartment on Sunday, two days from now. Yippee! I am super excited," she said, chirping.

I had given my word to Sarangi but how would I pull wool over the eyes of the society people and Ramu Kaka to let her in, only God knew. Not only that, there were more roadblocks. There are a thousand things in a bachelor's room that must be hidden before any girl can come over. You know what I mean. My room was no different from any bachelor's room, with food lying in the microwave, beer bottles in the kitchen and a dozen packets of Maggi and corn flakes on the dining table. A visit from Sarangi would mean that it needed to be in apple pie order. While tidying up the room was no big deal, the thorn in the flesh was Mr. Roy, my landlord.

Just so that you understand his notoriety, if any beer or whisky bottle was found in any of the bachelor boys' room, he would give a pain in the arse lecture to that boy. I wondered what would happen if he ever came to know that Sarangi visited my apartment. Firstly, don't call it an apartment, but a Nazi World War Two camp. Every time I used to open the door of my flat, I could sense him peeping from his door's keyhole. Aren't bachelors human beings? They have feelings too. All they want is to be loved and cared for. Anyway, there was no point in cussing Mr. Roy. Sarangi wanted to come on Sunday and I needed a robust plan to handle that A-class asshole, I mean, Mr. Roy.

The first step was to tidy up the apartment. I placed all the randomly-lying books in a new book shelf, gave my clothes to be ironed and sprayed some room freshener in each room. I bought two new bedsheets and spread them on the beds in each bedroom. Most of the tubelights in the apartment were fused and I replaced all of them. After a few hours, the house was given a complete facelift. The stepping task was done, but tricking Mr. Roy was still the deal breaker. I continued thinking throughout the day but no grand idea struck my mind. The next morning, while I was in deep sleep, an ear-piercing yell shook me awake. It was Mr. Roy screaming on the top of his voice at his servant Chandu, who was hardly two steps away.

"Dada, I am here only!" Chandu replied humbly. In the last three months, I had observed that he was a 'yes sir' servant.

"In the last month's society meeting, society committee had decided to install CCTV cameras at the front gate. There have been many thefts that have taken place in the neighbourhood. The society president had placed the order with Ghosla Electronics who rang me up this morning to tell me the CCTV cameras have arrived. Can you go and collect them now?" said Mr. Roy to Chandu in his apartment.

Hearing this, shit hit the fan. Sarangi wanted to come a day later, Sunday. Before I could figure out a plan handle the security guard Ramu kaka, Mr. Roy wanted to install CCTV cameras the day. Bitch! Everything was getting more complicated now.

With CCTV cameras installed, Mr. Roy could see who was entering the society, live! If there is a worse time for anything to go wrong, it will go wrong then. It was time to pull up my sleeves and get my act in place. I had to stop Chandu from getting the CCTV cameras, by hook or by crook. Before I could think any further, I saw Chandu stepping out of the society. In life, one has a choice to take one of the two paths: to wait for another better day, or to face it.

I locked the door of my apartment, did not bother taking the lift but instead ran down the three floors through the staircase. I started my bike and sped towards Ghosla Electronics. I passed Chandu on the way. He did not see me as he was walking slowly and talking on the phone. I reached Ghosla Electronics but had no clue of what I would say or how I'd stop Chandu. I entered the shop and it had lots of electronic items like LED TVs, air conditioners, music systems, etc., on display. There were a few salesmen standing too.

"I want to meet the owner urgently," I said to the one of the staff in the television section and he pointed towards one corner of the shop that had a small cabin with translucent glass. I walked swiftly towards that cabin.

"I am from Starwood Society" I said, trying to catch up with my breath.

"Yes, your Panasonic CCTV cameras have arrived. Can you wait for five minutes while I clear these customers?" said a seated bespectacled twenty-something guy, wearing a pink shirt. He naturally assumed that I was the authorized person from the society to collect the CCTV cameras.

"Don't take five minutes, you can take five days," I said.

"Good joke," he said, smiling and continuing to write something in the sales register.

"No, I am serious. I don't want you to deliver the cameras until Monday," I said, sounding serious while he looked dumbfounded.

"What? Mr. Roy just told me that he was sending someone and that I should keep them ready!" he said, confused.

"Yes, Chandu is coming to collect them. He is on the way," I said, telling the truth. On hearing this, he looked even more confused.

"Hold on! Hold on! If Chandu is the one who is going to collect them, who are you?" he asked.

"I am the person who doesn't want you to deliver them before Monday," I said pointedly.

"Man! What is happening? Mr. Roy says he wants them delivered and Chandu will collect them. Then you come from somewhere and tell me to deliver them on Monday. You have come and Chandu is also coming. I am lost!" he said. "Let me call Mr. Roy and find out what he wants. And by the way, may I know why you don't want them to get delivered today but only on Monday?" asked the terribly puzzled shop owner. Few other customers who were listening to the conversation also appeared fazed.

"My girlfriend is coming to my apartment this Sunday and if the CCTV cameras are delivered today, they will record her entry and I will be thrown out of the society," I said.

Honesty is mostly the best policy, unless you're posting a Facebook profile picture.

"Then why have you guys ordered them? I am still not getting it," said the puzzled shopkeeper.

"In Starwood Society, a girl's entry in a bachelor's apartment is considered a crime. That asshole...Sorry, I mean, Mr. Roy, is the landlord who has ordered the CCTV cameras and I am his tenant," I said.

"Okay. I get it now and he wants Chandu to collect them, while you don't want them to be delivered. Gotcha!" said the shop owner, finally understanding the situation.

There was silence in the shop for two minutes, but not long before he started to smile.

A smile is a curve that sets most things straight. I went ahead and hugged him. While a smile is the lighting system of the face, a hug is free roadside assistance.

"What do I get in return for not delivering the CCTV cameras today?" asked the almost laughing young shop owner.

"Buffet lunch and beer at Bar-B-Q Nation, Salt Lake!" I said, instantaneously offering him a pay-off.

"When do we go?" asked the shopkeeper, profoundly interested in the offer.

"Tomorrow? As soon as my girlfriend goes back, I will come over and pick you up from here," I said immediately.

"Done deal! Let Chandu come and I will tell him that the product is defective and needs replacement. I will tell him to come a month later. Till then, you can get your girlfriend inside a few more times," he said, and all the customers listening clapped in joy. It was the victory of truth and love. I almost kissed the shop owner in gratitude.

That roadblock was cleared but the road to Sarangi's entry in the society was still unresolved. Ramu Kaka was a tough, old time, loyal security guard of the society and used to make every visitor sign the security register before they could enter. I was back in my apartment and thinking hard on how to trick Ramu Kaka, when my doorbell rang. I peeped from the key hole. Raja and Ankur stood outside the door.

"Did you give your house a bath with Lifebuoy?" said both of them together, surprised at seeing the sparkling clean house.

"Guys, Sarangi is coming here tomorrow!" I said, spilling the beans.

"Wow! That is the reason behind the ultra-clean house. Ankur, you know, wine, women and wealth can get a man to do anything. Unfortunately, you and I have none of the three and that is why we are in this state!" said Raja.

"Have a good romantic date dude, but don't forget 'protection,'" he added.

Ankur giggled while I kept mum.

"Sir, the million dollar question is that how will Sarangi enter the building? Mr. Roy, Ramu Kaka...they certainly are the deal breakers in the way!" I asked, sounding worried. There was less than a day left and I had no clue on how it all would work out. Raja went to the kitchen, lit his cigarette and walked towards the balcony.

"I know how these two guys can be handled," said Raja, blowing smoke rings into the air, slowly.

"Before you sprout any master innovative idea, let me tell you, I don't want it to be as dreadful as the coffee plan at The Grand Vilas!" I said, getting jittery. I had been the victim in that fiasco and I didn't want a repeat performance of that.

"Guys, first understand that creatures like Mr. Roy cannot be tempted with a pay-off or bribe. The only way to bypass him is to get Sarangi in when he is not around. I have been analyzing him for almost three months, and if I am not wrong, he goes out for a stroll with Sylvester at nine in the morning," Raja said, slowly but with conviction while taking a deep puff inside.

"Who is Sylvester?" asked Ankur.

"His dog," I said, "not Sylvester Stallone, the Hollywood superstar."

Ankur giggled.

"That is step number one. Step two is that Ramu Kaka is the only other guy who can stall Sarangi's entry into the society," said Raja. A spark in his eyes indicated that he had an idea up the flagpole.

"He is an old timer here, guys, been here ever since the society was built. He is here from six in the morning till eleven at night. Not only that, he is very loyal to the society. He won't agree to my request of letting Sarangi in," I said frowning.

"Dude, do you know that loyalty has a price?" said Raja, grinning.

"What does that mean?" asked Ankur.

"It is not me, guys, I had read that Ambani had said these words. If you can find out the price with which you can manipulate Ramu Kaka, then the 'impossible' will, in no time, become 'possible'," Raja said, unveiling step two of the well-thought-through plan.

"Whenever I have gone for a smoke downstairs and have struck a conversation with Ramu Kaka, he appears to me as a financially challenged chap. He hardly gets to eat two proper meals a day, let alone good food," continued Raja in a thoughtful tone.

"Okay. So what has food got to do with Sarangi coming in?" I asked, trying to read Raja's mind.

"I have seen him drinking hooch and smoking cigarette leftovers that are thrown in the parking lot. So what we need to do is to get a dozen Kingfisher beer cans, few packets of Marlboro Lights cigarettes, two plates of fish fry and a plate of rice parcelled. Also, Bengali men love rasgullas more than their wives, so get him half a dozen of those as well," said Raja throwing a long but an ace plan that left Ankur and me eating our hats.

"If you do that, he will let Sarangi in; as many times as you want to, any day you want, with no song and dance!" said Raja, completing his statement and throwing the cigarette out of the balcony.

The plan definitely deserved a salute. Don't call it a plan but a roadmap. The difference between a plan and a roadmap is that the latter not only shows you the final destination but also a good way to get there.

All of us went downstairs to buy the stuff that Raja had recommended: Cans of Kingfisher beer, two packets of Marlboro Lights cigarettes, a fish fry meal and rasgullas. Seeing all of us with so much of food in our hands and walking towards him, Ramu Kaka seemed confused.

"Ramu Kaka, this is all for you!" I said, handing him all the stuff. "Thank you Sarthak, but what is the occasion?" asked a pleasantly surprised Ramu kaka.

"Ankur's father is getting married," Raja said with a dash of wit.

"What? My father!" said a startled Ankur, and all of us laughed.

"That was a joke, Ramu Kaka. This is for your selfless service to society for so many years, day and night, rain or sunshine," I said, flattering.

"Okay! But why today?" said Ramu Kaka hesitatingly. He didn't seem convinced with the sycophancy.

Raja, Ankur and I looked at one another. It was time to tell him the truth even though the truth is rarely simple in life. In life, we all need to be careful about whom we tell a secret as some people's way of keeping secrets these days is by posting it on Facebook. But befriending Ramu Kaka was important as he was the last roadblock in getting Sarangi in.

"There are some special guests coming tomorrow to my apartment. When they come in, please don't ask them any questions like 'who', 'why', etc. Also, don't force them to make any entry in the visitor register either. Just let them come inside with a smile!" I said to Ramu Kaka. He looked at me, grinning, and displaying wide his tobacco infested teeth in the process.

"Can I get this tomorrow as well? I promise, no one will come to know about your guests and no entry will be made in the register!" proposed Ramu Kaka, sounding desirous and looking tastefully at the beer bottles. For letting Sarangi in, I could buy him beer for an entire year, let alone for a day.

The CCTV dealer was befriended, Ramu Kaka was bribed and the house was in apple pie order. With Raja's master plan, the game was on! Raja and Ankur soon left. They had sorted my seemingly impossible problem. As they say, friends will fight with you daily for no reason, but whenever you are sad, they will fight with the world to end your sadness.

Early in the morning, my deep sleep was disturbed by a WhatsApp notification. It was still dark outside with the day almost breaking out. I looked at the watch and it showed four thirty in the morning.

"I will be in your apartment in less than five hours from now. Not getting any sleep and my mom is wondering what I am up to. Super excited...!" read the message and I smiled with my sleepy eyes.

Isn't it 'love' when the other person's happiness is more important than your own?

"See you shortly! Hugs," said the second message. I felt loved. To be loved is above all bargains. I managed to catch a few more hours of sleep but not for long as I heard Mr. Roy's earth-shaking voice.

"Chandu! Please take Sylvester out for a walk. I will join you in five minutes," I heard Mr. Roy telling Chandu. Sylvester Stallone, the Hollywood superstar, would have gone into major depression if he would have come to know that 'Sylvester' was a dog's name. Though Mr. Roy used to claim that it was a Labrador, Sylvester always appeared like a tail-wagging street dog to me. Soon the trio, Mr. Roy, Chandu and Sylvester, stepped out of Starwood Society for a walk, unintentionally creating an impeccable chance for Sarangi to sneak in.

Standing in the balcony of my third floor apartment, I was anxiously waiting with bated breath, wondering if Sarangi was anywhere near. I had my fingers crossed that Mr. Roy wouldn't change his mind and come back abruptly early from his dog walk. Sarangi, however, did not make me wait long as I saw her riding her Scooty towards my apartment. She was dressed in a sleeveless purple top with grey coloured jeans. She donned Ray-Ban aviators, with her black hair toppling over her shoulders. Stopping her Scooty at the society entrance, she looked up and smiled at me. I dialled her number.

"Park your Scooty in the two wheeler parking. There is a lift lobby on the right. Come to the third floor," I instructed on the phone. Seeing the gorgeous Sarangi, Ramu Kaka almost had a heart attack, but got a hold of himself, "Madam, please come in."

"There is no need to sign the register. Sarthak's flat is on the third floor, '3C'," said Ramu Kaka.

Sarangi was soon inside my apartment and I bolted the door from inside.

"Coming inside wasn't that tough!" Sarangi said, coming close and hugging me for long. She nuzzled my nose with hers and it felt like a dream.

"Shhh! Talk softly! I wish I could tell you what I had to do to get you here!" I said, smiling and looking into her eyes. She still had her arms around my neck, while we stared into each other's eyes.

I played Bryan Adams's song *Have you ever really loved a woman* on my laptop and we danced slowly for a while. When the love is greatest, the words are fewest.

"Wow! Nice room! Somehow it reminds me of our house in Lucknow when I was a five-year-old kid," she said, blushing and taking her arms off me.

"Dad and mom?" she asked, holding a photo frame that had mom and dad's photograph in Shimla – good old times when there was love between them.

"Yes, they are! Two out of the three people whom I love the most," I said, while she continued to gaze at the photograph. There was a blush on her face as she knew she was the third one.

"Your dad must have been a handsome hunk is his time!" she said, looking at the photograph.

"The wise say that the next generation is always more intelligent and smarter than the previous one!" I said, and she giggled.

"I am very good at making tea. People fall in love with the tea I make. Shall I make a cup for you now?" said Sarangi, placing the photo frame back on the shelf and walking towards the kitchen. Whether I would fall in love with the tea or not, I did not know, but I was surely in love with the charming tea maker.

"I have everything to make tea here, but can't see any sugar around," she said, all puzzled in the kitchen and looking for sugar while I just watched her. She looked even more beautiful when puzzled.

"Look for the sugar, not me!" she said, smiling. I looked beneath the bed and then in the refrigerator, as in a bachelor's den, common things are usually located in the most uncommon of places.

"Buddhu! How on earth will you find sugar beneath your bed? Go and get some from the shop downstairs!" she said, amused at my antics.

Truth be told, we were out of sugar last week and I ate my cornflakes with milk without sugar. May sound 'yuck', but I am just giving you an idea about the life of bachelors. We'd rather change our tastes than take the pain of going to the grocery store!

Half-heartedly, I locked the door from outside so that no one could get suspicious about Sarangi's presence in the house and went downstairs. It took me more than fifteen minutes to come back, and when I opened the door, Sarangi was sitting on the sofa waiting for me. There was however something different about the house. It looked like it had been arranged differently than when I had left. All the Maggi and cornflakes packets that were randomly lying in the kitchen were stacked properly inside the cabinet. The milk bottles lying in the hall were kept inside the refrigerator. Heaps of clothes that were on my bed were ironed and stacked in order. Someone has said it right that women are the real architects of society. When she had entered the house, she had hugged me only for few minutes, but now held my heart forever.

"Tea for you!" she said, handing me a hot cup and it tasted like the best thing on earth. It was a little too sweet, maybe it was her sweetness that was dissolved in it. Amidst our chatting, I finished my tea but unknowingly, continued sipping the empty cup. One cannot love and be sane.

"Buddhu, your cup is empty!" she said, taking it from me. Amidst our chatting, we never realized that time had raced to one in the afternoon and Mr. Roy was supposed to be back any time.

"Sarangi, that asshole, I mean Mr. Roy will be back any moment now! I don't want you to go but you must leave. If he sees us here, I will be forced to live either in jail or on a railway platform," I said, looking at her doe-like eyes. They had turned sad on hearing that she would need to go.

"Sure, my intelligent friend! Soon I will make chicken tikka masala for you. You have to taste the magic of my hands," she said, beaming, taking the cup back from me.

"I have a habit of licking fingers after good food," I said, she blushed and our souls felt connected. She hugged me, pecked on my right cheek and bid me goodbye.

"I think I deserved better," I said slowly, but loud enough to be heard.

She heard it, turned towards me and we kissed. Beauty is not skin deep, but sin deep. Where love is, there is faith. Being hugged and kissed by Sarangi was like worth three sessions of chemotherapy given to a cancer patient; *that* life infusing. We continued kissing passionately until we heard Mr. Roy's voice in the corridor.

"Chandu!" said Mr. Roy. Chandu was probably walking alongside him.

"Your landlord seems to be back! What do we do now?" asked a slightly anxious Sarangi. She still had her arms around my neck.

"He doesn't know you are here. Let us continue for a while until he disappears inside his house," I said. She closed her eyes and we continued kissing. Soon the noises in the corridor settled down and it was as calm as if no one had ever come since ages.

"Clean your lipstick marks before you go out," she said, smiling and rubbing my cheeks with her palm. I held her hand and kissed it again.

"I am going for a bath now. It is very hot outside!" said a loud voice from Mr. Roy's house and it was the perfect time for Sarangi to go downstairs. God is good. Both of us came down hurriedly. She started her Scooty and was about to go out of the society when Ramu Kaka said with a broad smile, "Please come again madam. Your visit made my day." Her visit had not only made Ramu Kaka's day, but my day too. Wherever you are, and whatever you do, be in love.

The Inescapable Destiny

⌘

The greatest physicist of modern times, Albert Einstein, once said: "Human beings, vegetables or cosmic dust, we all dance to a mysterious tune, intoned by an invisible piper." This chapter will tell you, life is what happens to you when you are busy making other plans. Little did I know that a traumatic time – the biggest challenge that one could ever face – was going to hit me soon. People around me say that being young is a victory in itself, but I doubt that. I was tired and nervous in my twenties in a way that I never am now. During that harrowing time, I would wonder how I was going to pull it off, but when I look back in time now, the feeling has been galactic. I will write more about that in a minute.

By now, I was a trusted face at Sarangi's place. Her parents were also at ease seeing us together. Where there is great love, there is faith. I had subtly mentioned about Sarangi to my mother back home in Delhi, but not to my dad as we had never spoken ever since I came to Kolkata. Sarangi and I were out shopping on one Sunday afternoon at Park Street and the plan was to go to McDonald's and then watch *Humpty Sharma ki Dulhania*. Sarangi loved the McChicken Kid's Meal at McDonald's as they would give a free soft toy with every order.

"Shall we go back home?" said Sarangi, after paying the bill for the saris that she had bought to be worn on her friend's wedding.

"Home? I thought we were going to McDonald's and then for a movie. No?" I said rather surprised as we had made a different plan an hour back.

"Don't know. I am feeling fatigued and feverish since afternoon," she said. I touched her forearm and it was warmer than usual.

"Why didn't you tell me this earlier? We wouldn't have come down today. Let us go home. We will see the movie some other day!" I said, putting her shopping bags in the back seat of my Santro.

"You see how this weather is changing. Half of my office is out sick!" I said, touching her forehead that felt warm. We got a take away from McDonald's.

"The burger is yummy, try it with coke!" she said, putting a small piece into my mouth as I had my hands behind the wheel.

"Yes, good…! Before you sleep tonight, take one spoonful of your dad's brandy and you will be back up and kicking by morning," I said, taking a sip of the coke that she was holding.

"In my college days, just to get that thrill of doing something illegal, I would slowly finish my dad's brandy but would continue refilling it with water. One day, I heard my dad saying that the brandy was bland and must have expired," I said and she smiled, but with unease.

Over these last three months, she had developed immense trust in me. I loved her. I guess she loved me too. But none of us had said anything to each other, out of fear of rejection and getting hurt. I stepped on the pedal of the car as I wanted her to reach home and rest as soon as possible.

"Aunty, did Sarangi tell you that she is not feeling well? She has got high fever," I said, holding her hand and helping her into the house.

"Nothing Mom, Sarthak is panicking for no rhyme or reason. You see how this weather is changing daily – one day humid and the second day it's scorching hot!" said Sarangi, trying to assure her mother, who by now was a bag of nerves.

"Can you make me some vegetable soup for dinner? Won't be able to eat much as I had two burgers," said Sarangi, sitting on the sofa. What she had told her mom was far from the truth. She had fed me both the burgers while I was driving and she herself had a few bites. Her mother, however, could sense that Sarangi wasn't well. A mother is a mother, who can see and hear what the child does not share.

"Aunty, please add some black pepper to it. It will make the soup taste better and will kill the viral infection faster," I said, while her mother went inside the kitchen. My mother in my childhood use to feed me soup with black pepper whenever I had fever. I wanted Sarangi to recover quickly. I was concerned, but not that much. With the early arrival of the monsoon, there was a sudden change in the weather and most probably, it was viral fever. She wanted to sleep so I left for my apartment.

The next day, I called her.

"I had a hundred and five fever that fluctuated many times in the night. Dad will be taking me to Goodlands Hospital," said Sarangi, sounding fatigued. I felt gutted. A hundred and five degrees did not sound very normal.

"Don't know why my parents are so nervous. I am sure the doctor will give me some paracetamol tablets. Hey, by the way, there is a weekend sale at South City Mall. Let us go and do some shopping the coming Sunday," she said, sounding excited, but with a bit of discomfort in her voice.

I nodded but kept wondering about the fever. Later in the day, I spoke to Sarangi's dad and came to know that their family physician had recommended some advanced blood tests and an MRI scan to be done. Sarangi's father was a retired army lieutenant who had been felicitated with a bravery award by the President of India, but when it came to his own daughter, he sounded nervous.

"Things seem more complex than viral fever or malaria," said Sarangi's dad, sounding tense over phone.

Hearing this, I felt disoriented and couldn't focus on my work. As they say, love is full of fears. I got up from my desk and sought Rajan's permission to leave early and went straight to Sarangi's home.

"I don't understand why everyone is talking crazy!" I said to Sarangi's mother. I was very upset.

While talking to her family, I observed Sarangi's dad and it occurred to me that he knew something that the rest of us did not. Sarangi was resting on her bed and I pulled a chair to sit by her side. She wanted to talk, but I put my finger on her lips as I wanted her to recover soon. After spending a few hours, and waiting till she finally fell asleep, I came back to my apartment. The next day in the morning before going to office, I wanted to see Sarangi and drove to her home.

Her dad was sitting on the sofa with a bunch of papers in his hand, with his head bowed down. There was something wrong with his body language.

"What happened, uncle? What are these papers that you are holding in your hand?" I asked out loud from the door, dumbfounded and scared, as I had never seen a stalwart army man so blue. He appeared frozen and did not answer.

"What is wrong, uncle? What do the test reports say?" I asked, coming close to him and shaking him by his shoulders. I looked towards Sarangi's room and guessed she must be sleeping with the lights off and the door half shut.

He kept mum but handed me the bunch of reports that he was holding. I flipped through them, but couldn't understand much of the medical terms.

"What do these reports say?" I asked, freaking out as he was looking down.

"Sarangi has been diagnosed with terminal stages of leukaemia, a form of cancer," said Sarangi's father, sobbing and breaking down at his feet.

"Leukemia? Cancer...Do you understand what you are saying?" I asked breathless. I felt as if someone had hit me very hard in the stomach. Sarangi being diagnosed with cancer was unimaginable. What appeared to be a plain viral fever two days back was actually a dormant monster of life-threatening cancer? From this point on, a rollercoaster journey will start that will narrate how far one can go to save his love. Be with me.

"I am sure there is some mix up somewhere. Either the reports have gotten exchanged with someone else's or it has been diagnosed incorrectly. Terminal stage leukaemia is just not possible!" I said, hopping mad at the sudden turn of mind-boggling events.

I went inside Sarangi's room and she was sleeping unperturbed. I touched her forehead and it appeared abnormally cold to me. Something was not right. Just a few days back, we had gone out to Park Street and now there was this horrifying news. I rushed out of the house, started my bike and raced it to the maximum towards the hospital where Sarangi's reports had come from. I rode rashly, and even on the wrong side of the road, but did not care. I jumped a few red lights and reached the hospital in less than ten minutes and stopped my bike at the gate. It fell down, but I didn't bother, and ran inside. Nothing was as important as Sarangi's life at that point in time.

"Can I talk to Dr. Biswas, the oncologist?" I said, panicking and catching my breath.

"I am sorry sir, the doctor has left for the day," said the receptionist politely, looking at how breathless I was.

"You guys have messed up some reports. I need to talk to the doctor urgently," I yelled.

People sitting in the waiting area kept turning their heads at me, but I did not care. When life gives you desperate measures, one is free to act as desperately as he wants. Seeing me batty, the receptionist called the doctor who apparently was driving.

"Dr. Biswas, sorry to bother you, but this is Sarthak here, Sarangi Sen's friend, whose reports say that she has been diagnosed with leukaemia!" I said panting. I badly wanted to hear from him that the reports had somehow been mixed up.

"Yes, she has been diagnosed with leukaemia, terminal stages," said the doctor on the other side of the phone, unruffled. The very nature of the medical profession makes the physician unattached to patients, and unaffected by such emotions.

"Are you sure reports have not gotten exchanged with any other patient? She was just fine a few days back!" I asked in a tizzy.

"For the cases that show up critical values, we repeat the test thrice, just to be sure. The same procedure is being followed in Sarangi's case also. Therefore, the chance of error in tests or reports mixing up is zero," the doctor said, unflustered, and with that statement of his, I didn't have a leg to stand on.

"Jesus! Then what is the treatment path from here? I know you are driving, but I need to know this," I asked anxiously, while sweating profusely.

Dr. Biswas, one of the most renowned oncologists in Kolkata had the reputation of bringing the most seemingly impossible cases back to life.

"Sarthak, I must tell you in clear words that in her case, chances of recovery are minimal from this stage onwards, and that is why I am calling it a 'terminal stage'. We can start chemo and administer strong painkillers, but unfortunately, it is curtains time for her. I have told the same thing to her father!" said the doctor, slowly.

I screamed on the phone feeling crushed under the mighty design of God.

"Maybe she will survive for three months at the most, but her health will deteriorate fast. Feel free to get second opinions at Tata Memorial, Mumbai or Christian Medical College, Vellore," said the doctor before hanging up.

My mind had gone numb. Life is what happens while you are busy making other plans. I was starting to see the ugly face of destiny emerging. We find the predictable boring, but in real life, the unpredictable is mostly terrifying. Love is probably the most beautiful thing you can have, and the most painful thing you can lose. Only now, a year later, can I see how I was running on nervous energy. The destiny was no lesser than Goliath and I was vulnerable at that point of time.

I came out wiping my tears to the visitor's parking lot. I wondered if destiny could really be so unforgiving to a vivacious girl like Sarangi. I drove straight to her house, went inside her room; she was awake and I hugged her. I was devastated from within, but swallowed my desire to cry. Two things however can't be hidden: love and tears. She knew that something was up.

"What happened? You look sad!" she said, moving her hand through my hair. She was still lying on the bed and looked pale.

"Just a bad day at office!" I said, holding her hand, while she continued running her fingers through my hair.

"Don't worry. Bad days don't last for long. There will be sunshine soon," she said, tapping my cheek.

"I hope so too!" I said, but was feeling shattered after what Dr. Biswas had told me.

I left her home, painfully distressed, around 8.00 p.m. and came back to my apartment, but couldn't sleep. The next day, I opened my eyes to a so-called 'new day'. I felt like closing them again, knowing that the day would only bring bad news. When the best oncologist in the town had said that she had only three months to live, what chances of survival did she have? Why would a loveable and affectionate person like her suffer a fate like this? I was alone, sad and I had come to the end of my rope.

In the next two days, me and her father scanned all the reports and sent them to one of the doctors at a leading cancer hospital in Mumbai. I was not going to give up so easily against the unkind invisible script of destiny. Testing, trying, adverse and painful times lay ahead. If we were to beat this ugly script of destiny, we had to get ahead of ourselves. I had to become bigger than what I was, more courageous and greater in spirit. Her father was with me in my apartment.

"Uncle, I have come to know of a brilliant oncologist in California. He is my colleague's dad. The medical science in the US is far advanced than other countries, and I am sure he will be able to help us in this trying time," I said, trying to reassure him and probably myself too. Hope is a poor man's bread.

"Sarthak, we need to save Sarangi in the little time that we have. I don't know why, but God has not been fair to us," said Sarangi's father, almost breaking down.

I tried calming him, while I myself had no clue about why there was such a painful destiny scripted for Sarangi. From nowhere, we were up against something too strong, too mighty to beat. The unfortunate part of this mysterious script of destiny is that you can only feel it as it happens to you, but you can't see the next page.

From my office, I scanned all the reports and emailed them to Dr. Pratik Sharma, the father of my engineering college's roommate and a renowned oncologist in New Jersey, United States of America. I called him late in the night as well and requested him to do his best. He promised to go through the reports and revert within a couple of days. Everything that is done in the world is done by hope, but sometimes, hope is only a good breakfast and a bad supper. In this melee, three more days had passed, but there was no response from Dr. Pratik.

After a busy day in office, I had hardly entered my apartment when I noticed an email alert on my phone. I looked at the screen and it was from Dr. Pratik. My heart skipped a beat as his email was going to be a make or break deal. I crossed my fingers and looked up at God before opening the email.

'Dear Sarthak, thank you for your email and the scanned reports of Sarangi. I have gone through them and unfortunately, this is a very advanced stage case. Not only are the chances of survival almost nil in this case, but also the patient, in my opinion, is left with a life of not more than three months. I am sure your Indian doctors have told you the

same thing as well. I am sorry to say that I will not be able to help much in this case. Hope everything else is fine in your family. Say hello to your dad for me.

Thanks, Dr. Pratik Sharma.

King Norman Medical Institute of Oncology, California, United States of America.

This email spelt a calamity and my soul was injured. How could God, the so-called creator of the world, be so tough on an innocent and vibrant Sarangi? I lacked the courage to break the news to Sarangi's family, as her father, with all the doors seeming closed, had all his hopes pinned on Dr. Pratik. I sat down on the sofa as I felt dizzy and passed out.

In some time, I regained consciousness. It was not a time to weep or curse my stars, but to act. We had little time in hand and had to find out something, someone to save Sarangi. Action doesn't always bring happiness, but there will not be any happiness without action. In a few minutes, you will read about the indomitable spirit that was displayed in the circumstances, the mere thoughts of which can send shivers down the spines of ordinary men and women.

I got up from the sofa, logged on to my laptop and researched about the disease and its survival path. Eight hours of pursuit on Google indicated a gloomy path forward. I felt fatigued and exasperated. Trying to save your loved ones when all the doors seemed closed can be the biggest challenge ever that one can face in life. I dialled Sarangi's phone; it kept ringing for a while before she picked up.

"Hey, how are you? You took a long time," I said as normally as I could.

"First tell me what has happened to me, malaria or viral? Mom, Dad, no one is telling me!" she said, sounding annoyed.

"Doctor says it is some sort of allergy!" I lied.

White lies are a part of everyday life. If they can make someone feel better, they are not bad. Our courtship was on for almost a year now. Between us, it was requited love, but unconfessed. Given her state of health, I didn't have much time in my hand to tell her how much I loved her. I decided to confess it as it would surely bring a smile on her face. Being someone's first love is good, but being someone's last love is soul enriching. I thought of proposing to Sarangi in my own special way.

I rode towards her house. There was a famous gold jewellery shop on the way to her home, Keshav Chandra Agarwal Jewellers, also known in the city as KC Jewellers. It was already 9.00 p.m. when I stopped my bike in front of the shop that had half its shutters down.

"I need to buy a ring," I went straight to the counter and asked one of the salesmen who was busy writing something in the sales register.

"Sir, we are almost closed. I won't be able to show you all the designs but only the ones that are still outside!" answered a guy from the back, dressed in a suit. He appeared to be KC himself with the authority that he was displaying. I nodded because I didn't have a choice as the shop.

"Her name starts with 'S'. Can you show me something with that letter?" I requested.

"Lucky fellow…! Here is one which we have not put back in the safe and it has 'S' embossed on it. Fifteen thousand…!" said KC, showing me a white coloured ring.

"Lovely. I will take this," I said, imagining how stunning it would look on Sarangi's finger.

"Okay. Your credit card please," said KC, readying the credit card swiping machine.

I slid my hand in my pocket but couldn't feel the wallet there. That was odd. I cautiously checked all the pockets again and still couldn't find it in any one of them. Gosh! I recollected in time that I had accidently forgotten it at home.

"Need your credit card sir! The shop is about to be closed," said KC, getting restless and waiting for my credit card.

I was in a spot. KC had shown me a ring that I wanted, but I didn't have the money. This forgetting of the wallet was a serious piece of bad luck. Every moment in life is worth infinite possibilities and the charm of our destiny is that it moves in a mysterious way. In life, you can never tell whether bad luck may after all turn out to be good luck. Continue reading.

"KC, how do I tell you this? I have left my wallet at home but I need to buy this ring today. Be rest assured, I will hand you the money tomorrow first thing before your shop opens," I pleaded.

"Sorry boss, we don't deal with credit or promises!" said KC, clearly mad. He had shown me the ring that I wanted even when the shop was closing and embarrassingly I did not have money.

"Guys, put that ring back in the safe and don't allow anyone to enter the shop after 9.00 p.m. from tomorrow. All sorts of weird characters come at this hour!" said a spiked up KC to his sales boy.

"Sir, please, you may leave now!" said KC sternly. The entire staff in the shop had perceived that I was not a serious buyer.

Bargaining is the last thing one should attempt with Marwari businessmen and here I was requesting him to give me a ring based on a promise.

"Listen mister, don't waste my time. Security, can you throw this good for nothing fellow out of the shop, right now?" said the furious KC, and before I could think of anything, two security guards came close and told me go out of the shop.

"Keep my iPhone and my bike that is parked outside this shop. Once you get your money tomorrow, only then will I collect the bike and the phone from you. They will be more than double the cost of the ring I have selected. You don't know this but this ring will be for someone who may not see light of day after two months," I said aloud while being dragged out of the shop.

KC heard clearly what I had said. From being livid a few seconds ago, his body language seemed better. I was almost out the shop being dragged by guards.

"KC, you know what, ditch it! You won't get it unless you have truly loved someone," I shouted from the door.

"There was a girl…," came out the words from KC's mouth, and the entire staff was stunned upon hearing this.

"Sorry, that was a slip of the tongue! Guards, leave the boy for a minute. Let me understand what he is saying!" instructed KC to his staff. His confession had revealed some shades of his past but he was a smart guy; he changed the topic. Someone has said it right, love is contagious and no matter how hard you try, you can't hide it.

"What is this bike and phone deal that you are trying to strike with me?" asked KC pointedly, but with a mellowed down tone.

"KC, my girlfriend whom I want to propose to with this ring, has been diagnosed with leukaemia, a type of cancer. You keep my bike and phone which is more than the cost of ring. I will be at your shop first thing tomorrow morning with the cash. I want to tell her that I love…" I said, pausing and choking half way through. KC gestured me to stop.

"What do you do?" asked KC, better in composure, but in thoughts.

"I work for NetCon Consulting in Sector V," I said.

"Did you say NetCon?" he asked. "My brother was a director there until last month. He quit the job and manages our store at Rajarhat," said KC. "Let me find out from Bhai if he knows you. If things look good, then this is the first and possibly the last time I would give anyone a ring on credit!" said KC, taking out his phone.

"Is your brother Ram Chandra Agarwal? He used to head NetCon's India sales division." I asked. Ram Chandra Agarwal was a vice president in NetCon and a big farewell was arranged when he had resigned.

"Okay! So you know him. That is good, but let me still talk to him," he said dialling a number on his phone. While dialling the number, he was gazing at my feet. I looked down and I had created a blooper in my rush. I had a Reebok jogger on my left foot and leather Bata sandals on the right one. Wearing two different sandals, with no card or cash, I was trying to get a ring on a promise. Certain situations in life can't be described in words.

He was still on a call with his brother at a distance from me.

"My brother thinks he knows you and that is good for now!" he said, disconnecting the call and stepping towards me. His body language revealed a lot. The face is the mirror of the mind, and eyes without speaking can confess the feelings of the heart.

"Keep your phone and bike with you, I won't keep them. But you can take the ring for now and give me the money tomorrow," he said, and I heaved a sigh of relief. The things that I learnt that day were that relationships are complex, outcomes are uncertain, people are irrational, but if the intent is good, things fall into place.

"One more thing, from next time onwards, please wear the same type of shoes before you go shopping," said KC, smiling.

This sudden turn of events where a Marwari businessman, known to be a tough taskmaster, showed his compassionate human side, had amazed me. Someone had said it right, a prayer from a true heart brings all the forces in the universe together to fulfil its wishes.

"Thank you sir, you have no clue what you have done for me! I will be here with the money first thing in the morning tomorrow," I said, thanking him for his gratitude, despite being a stranger to him.

"And you also have no clue what I have done to myself in front of my whole staff!" he said, referring to the slip of tongue in which he accidently admitted his crush on a girl.

I left the shop with the ring and a promise to pay back before noon. I was about to start my bike when my phone rang. It was Sarangi.

"Sarthak, where are you?" asked Sarangi. There was unease and fatigue in her voice; worried as I had not reached, fatigued as she was not well.

I told her I am on the way, and she continued. "Papa is unable to find one of his leather sandals since yesterday. Strangely there is a Reebok jogger lying in the shoe rack outside the house."

"I am also wearing a Reebok Jogger and a Bata leather sandal!" I said, confessing and she giggled. Her chuckles were soothing as I had heard them after a very long time.

"I had the intuition that it would be the work of my absent minded intelligent friend," she said, twittering.

There wasn't much traffic on the road and I reached her house in no time.

"Sarangi is in her room, but awake. I saw her smiling after weeks now," said her mother, hiding her tears. Those tears were a mix of happiness and sorrow, as Sarangi had smiled after a long time, but she was slowly drifting towards the inevitable.

"Hey, what's up!" I said, trying to cheer her up. I had the ring from KC in my pocket. Sarangi and I were in her room. The adjoining room had her mother as well as a person from the diagnostic laboratory, who had come down to collect some blood samples. Blood tests were, however, a mere formality at this time, if one was to go by the doctor's opinion. I had a thousand thoughts running wild in my mind. It wasn't the best ambience for a proposal, with people in the next room. But isn't life worthwhile only when you live without fear, love without limits, dream without boundaries and believe without doubt?

"What is on your mind?" she asked with a naughty smile on her face.

Love speaks even when lips don't say much.

I bent down on my knees with the ring in my hand, looking into her eyes.

"The day I will go on my knees for another girl, is the day I will tie a shoe lace for you or my daughter. Will you marry me?" I asked, looking into her eyes. She kept looking at me and soon tears started rolling from her eyes.

"Do you know that I will not be there after three months?" she said and I was struck with a lightning of thousand volts. All this while we were all trying to conceal the reality from her on pretexts of viral or weather change, but she knew it all. She still had tears rolling down, but it occurred to me that they were tears of joy.

"I will not let anything happen to you. Will you marry me?" I said slowly. As they say, love may go hit stone walls, but will ultimately find its way.

"Yes, I will," she said, sitting on the bed and extending her hand.

I slid it onto her ring finger. She hugged me sitting on the bed and I could feel her tears falling on my shirt. Her hair still smelled the same, just as it did when I had met her for the first time. I left for home soon after. I had the task of saving Sarangi to fulfil with buoyancy and grit. I had to become bigger than what I was – in courage, in spirit. I had to be victorious. The times that lay ahead reminded me of the words of Sir Winston Churchill – It is victory, victory at all costs, victory in spite of all terror, victory, however long and hard the road may be; for without victory, there is no survival.

How does a young boy with no knowledge of medical science play dice with Sarangi's destiny. That too when even the leading oncologists in the world concluded that her number was up? Would Sarthak be able to alter Sarangi's script of fate and save his love or, would he let Sarangi succumb to the design of mighty destiny? A wise man once said that in every imaginable situation there's the perfect shot: it could be through a glass or from behind someone's head. The job is to find it. That's my instinct, and it's an instinct I love in other people. All this and more, I will let you know in a minute.

A Journey Against all Odds

⌘

Every passing day was a nightmare with Sarangi's health deteriorating and complex symptoms flaring up. When medical science closes its door, what are the options one is left with? I had to find a solution in these trying circumstances. I am often called arrogant, and I suppose, I must be – but you might have to be arrogant in order to challenge certain deals when you don't deserve them. Sarangi's life did not deserve one such deal and we had to find someone who could save her. Who would it be? What would you have done if you were ever caught in such an abysmal situation? My default position in life has always been to hope that the impossible is only the impossible until your imagination proves otherwise. However, I was learning to deal with the pain every day and it had started to show on my health. I had not shaved for almost two weeks now and had not been eating properly. I don't know if I was on Asperger's or eccentric or whatever, but I know I was single-minded at that point of time. Amidst all this, I had forgotten to call my parents too. I had forgotten another thing: to repay KC for the ring and it would come back to bite me soon. Be with me.

My credit card bills were piling up as I was buying Sarangi's medicines, the little that I could do for her. With every passing day, I was going to bed with the hope that God would be kind to Sarangi. The next day in office, as soon as I entered, I saw Rajan in front of me.

"What's wrong with you, Sarthak?! Come to my room," said Rajan, and I followed him. One could easily guess that I was disturbed a great deal as Sarangi's health had become the main pre-occupation of my life. I began narrating the whole story to him from our courtship days to the state she was in, how she was diagnosed and the doctor's verdict. Rajan seemed up the pole on hearing the narration. He was of course concerned. I had heard numerous stories about him on how he, being from a son of a vegetable seller, rose to become the vice president at NetCon Consulting at the age of thirty-nine. Little do we know that the most intelligent people are those who have known defeat, known suffering, known struggle, known loss, and have found their way out of the depths. But here, unfortunately in front of God's script, human intelligence, persistence or courage stands little chance. As a wise man once said – "A human being in front of the invisible script of God is like a little child entering a huge library filled with books in many languages. The child knows someone must have written those books. It does not know how. It does not understand the languages in which they are written. The child dimly suspects a mysterious order in the arrangements of the books, but doesn't know what it is."

"Sarthak, I am no doctor, but in your life you will face many such perplexing situations. The true test of a man's character is not how he lives in good times, but how he fares in bad times. Keep searching until you have found a solution. If one solution doesn't work, look for another. Continue your zest and one day you will surely find one," said Rajan firmly.

Before he could say anything else, his desk phone started ringing. To my surprise, he disconnected the call. Two human beings were talking at this point, not a manager and a reportee.

"Sarthak, I strongly believe that when man closes one door, God opens two. I have personally seen many such situations where things come back to full life from the middle of nowhere. It is just that you need to keep going and never give up. Almost all the time, success is very near when we tend to give up," Rajan said to me.

His words were soothing, but the time was running out. I was reaching the end of the rope, but I wanted to tie a knot and hang on. One day, I reached home well past 11.00 p.m. and saw Mr. Roy, my landlord, who was out for a walk after dinner with Sylvester.

"Sarthak, your grandfather had called from Chandigarh. He wasn't getting through to your number and he has asked me to tell you to call him back," he said.

My grandfather had spent most of his life in Chandigarh, a beautiful city in northern India. I got into my apartment and called him at once.

"Grandpa, sorry I have not called you for quite a while," I said, feeling guilty.

"Sarthak, are you doing well these days? Why does something tell me that everything is not alright," he asked and I felt choked with emotions. God could not be everywhere and so he made grandparents. I was tired and nervous at that time, in a way that I had never been. I was observing the strain of trying to save Sarangi against the invisible script. I took a deep breath, and started narrating to him the turbulent series of events.

"You have always bought me ice-cream when I used to cry as a child. Can you tell me where can we get that ice-cream that will make everyone smile?" I said, and he sensed the helplessness in my voice.

There was a long silence on the phone. "You there, Grandpa?" I asked.

"I might not know of a doctor, but there is a person who can guide you in such distressing times," he said with conviction in his voice.

"Really? Oh my God! Why didn't we speak earlier! Who is he? A doctor? A naturopath? A homeopath? Or, an ayurvedic doctor? Or, a patient who has survived this holocaust?" I asked, as I had a thousand questions running in my mind, without any answers. A call to him had brought a ray of sunshine.

"He is not a doctor, but he has helped many like you in similar intricate situations that have no visible solutions at hand," he said with the same conviction.

"If he is not a doctor, then how can he be of any help? Sorry Grandpa, but I am not in a state to discuss anything that is only philosophical and not worthwhile," I said to him and hung up. I knew I was rude but when you have an injured soul, it is tough to be polite. I locked my apartment and went back to Sarangi's house at around 9.00 p.m.

"Papa has put a TV in my room. Sony Max is showing *Dilwale Dulhaniya Le Jayenge*," she said, with heaviness in her voice.

"You will be fine soon and then all of us – you, me, Raja and Ankur – will go to Digha. I have a few holidays in October for Durga Puja," I said trying to cheer her up. Digha is a sea-facing small town around four hours away from Kolkata.

"Why spoil the fun by taking along Raja and Ankur? It will be just you and me," she said with a smile that seemingly had visible pain. I smiled then, but later went to the other room, locked it and cried. What means could I have used to save her from the clutches of death? When science says all the doors are closed for you, does it really mean curtains? I sat for some time with her father and came back gutted around midnight. Sarangi's family was not only distressed from their daughter's deteriorating health, but also from the huge expenses incurred for various tests, reports and medicines.

Our destiny moves in a mysterious way. Things start happening when we think they are farthest off. Next morning, my phone buzzed and it was Rajan calling.

"Sarthak, I just wanted to know how your friend is doing," asked a busy but caring Rajan.

"Not good Rajan, still very unwell. There doesn't seem to be a way out," I said in the dumps. I had applied for loss of pay leave so he was not expecting me to be in the office at least for the next few days.

"How is the family handling the finances for the treatment? As far as I know, cancer treatment is very expensive," said Rajan. He was correct. Cancer treatment is indeed financially draining.

"I think it has caused a big dent in the family's savings. I am trying to contribute the best I can as well," I said, as daily expenditure on tests, medicines and reports was running up to more than twenty thousand rupees a day. Unfortunately, illness comes with no budget.

"Okay, so here is what I have done. I was out to Chicago last month but made time to send an e-mail to the worldwide employees of NetCon Consulting to contribute for your friend's cause, and don't worry, I have maintained your friend's privacy," Rajan said, and I continued listening to him in awe.

"The total money that NetCon employees have contributed is around six lakhs thirty thousand. In addition, I saved close to two lakhs on this US trip and I would want to contribute that from my side. My wife wanted a diamond ring, but that can wait," he added.

I was amazed at this unfamiliar human side of his personality. He was known to be a tough taskmaster, but it occurred to me that he also wanted Sarangi to win this battle. I thanked him for his compassion. That evening I left work overwhelmed, with a deep sense of gratitude.

✠

"Chhotu, give me one egg roll and tea," I said to the shop boy outside Starwood Society, but my mind was elsewhere. I was beginning to pace up and down. Like a panther in a cage, I was looking for an outlet for action. Waiting for Chhotu to get me the tea, I tried recollecting the conversation I had had with my grandfather two days ago. During the course of our conversation, he had mentioned a person who was not a doctor but could help me. My grandfather was a very wise and experienced person who couldn't have said such things randomly, especially after knowing my state. I felt that calling him again was the right thing to do.

"When we spoke last time, you said you know a person who could help," I said to my grandfather, coming straight to the point.

"Yes, he may be able to help, but he is not a doctor. Didn't you say that you wouldn't need his help?" he said. I think he felt bad as I had been rude the last time.

"If that person is not a doctor, how can he help a cancer patient?" I argued logically. I wanted to know the details.

"How he will help I can't say, but given that all doors seem closed, I think he will be able to offer some comfort. When I was your age, he on multiple instances, helped me come out of some difficult situations," he said with conviction in his voice.

"You turned ninety-seven this year in April. He must be really aged…but nonetheless, who and where is he?" I asked, flabbergasted. If I was to believe my grandfather, this person would be more than a hundred years old.

"Unfortunately, I cannot tell you more about him, but I can give you his address if you wish to go and seek his advice," he said.

With no leg to stand on and nervous with an ongoing one-sided battle, I did not have the energy to argue any further. I noted down the address of this enigmatic person. It was an address in Rishikesh, a small yet beautiful town in the foothills of the Himalayas in northern India. It is also known as the gateway to the Garhwal Himalayas.

"When do you plan to go?" he asked calmly.

"As early as possible! May be day after tomorrow," I said, as Sarangi was living on borrowed time.

"After you have travelled for two hours from Delhi to Rishikesh, on the highway you will see a Sardarji ka Dhaba. Try stopping there for your lunch. Besides the good food, you will learn some important lessons of life," he said with a voice that oozed tranquillity.

While he did not answer my question of how would that person help, it was for the first time someone trustworthy had said that there was hope. I logged on to the internet and bought two tickets from an online travel planner – one for Raja and one for myself. A day before travelling to Rishikesh, I drove to Sarangi's house to see her. She was sleeping in her room; I gently kissed her forehead and came out into the hall to meet her father who was sitting on the sofa with big lines of worry etched deep on his forehead. It was a no brainier to guess that they had appeared owing to his daughter's health as well as his finances getting drained.

"How do you reckon tomorrow will be like, uncle?" I asked Sarangi's dad just to pick up a conversation.

"Sarthak, I have to go to the bank tomorrow morning to get another fixed deposit released as more money will be required for medicines," he said, stressed out.

"Uncle, you are going to the bank tomorrow not to get any fixed deposit released, but to encash these cheques of six lakhs and two lakhs respectively that my company has arranged for Sarangi's treatment. They have also told me that if more money is needed, they will try and arrange it," I said diligently taking out the cheques that Rajan had given me.

Sarangi's father was moved. For the first time, he felt that he wasn't alone in this trying time. There were twenty thousand employees of NetCon supporting him, wanting him to win this battle. As they say, life is not as good as you believe it is, but also not as bad as it seems.

"But I also want to tell you something important – don't think that if Dr. Biswas says her time is up, we give up hope completely. I have just come to know of someone who could help us," I said, feeling hopeful after having spoken to my grandfather.

"Really! But all the doctors including those in the US have said she has zero chances of survival!" asked a slightly puzzled, but emotional father.

"I still don't know how that person can help, but his recommendation has come from a very trustworthy person," I said. "I don't want to give you too much hope but I don't want to regret that we did not try enough. That person is in Rishikesh and I am going there tomorrow."

Every time we witness something that we don't deserve, we train our character to be passive and thereby lose all our ability to defend us and our loved ones. I had this strange confidence in me that the game was far from over. I stood defiant but ill-equipped. You have to get over your own need for reassurance and resist the comfort zone of knowing you're only doing what others have done or are doing around you. Great results can't be achieved like that.

My flight to Dehradun was at six in the morning and it meant we needed to be at the airport by five. I hired a prepaid cab to reach Raja's house by three in the morning. I rang the bell and perceptibly no one opened the door for a while. I pressed the bell a few more times and soon there were movements in the house and a few lights were switched on. Raja's dad opened the door.

"Sarthak, you, at this hour? Hope everything is alright," said Raja's father, groggy. He tried looking at his watch but couldn't see in the dark.

"Raja and I have a 6.00 a.m. flight to Dehradun via Delhi today!" I said, fumbling. When you don't have a story to tell, you fumble.

"Really! For what? Raja never told me about this? He is sleeping like a log!" he said dumbfounded.

"My company has opened a new office in Delhi and there are walk-in interviews today. They have shortlisted his profile. If Raja clears it, he can get a job and then later on we can try to get him transferred back to Kolkata," I said a white lie at the drop of the hat and his father seemed persuaded.

Shortly, Raja and I were at the Netaji Subhash Chandra Bose Airport in Kolkata.

I felt I was in preparation for something. I had started a journey that would change my belief for a long time to come and in a few minutes from now, yours too. Shortly I will tell you what I felt like at that point. Sometimes, late in the night I would feel some invisible force telling me not to give up. At some time, that invisible force has its own quiet way to communicate with you. This journey would prove to be the link that made possible the future I had hoped for. I was neither so ambitious nor so capable, but I knew I was onto something that felt right. Life on the run had begun again in earnest, and it would not stop for a long time.

Rishikesh – Gateway to the Himalayan Shrine

⌘

Ifell asleep as soon as the plane took off while Raja got busy talking to a good looking airhostess. After a little more than two hours, our flight landed at the Indira Gandhi International Airport in New Delhi and we hired a prepaid Innova outside the departure gate. The cab started cruising towards Rishikesh and we instructed the cab driver to stop at Sardarji ka Dhaba. Truth be told, it was a bizarre recommendation from by my grandfather, given my objective was to go to Rishikesh.

"We have arrived at Sardarji ka Dhaba," said the driver, slowing down.

Both Raja and I stepped out and walked towards that dhaba. It had small open air bamboo huts – at least a hundred of them, with tables and chairs arranged inside them. It was crowded but what was the thing that my grandfather wanted me to learn at that dhaba?

"Come in my boys. I am glad that you have got a table, usually one has to wait for at least thirty minutes," said a voice from somewhere behind us. We turned around to see a well-built, fair stalwart of a Sardarji. His black kurta pajama matched his turban and with the confidence that he oozed, he appeared to be the owner of the dhaba.

"Where are you guys coming from?" he asked, calmly walking towards us.

"From Kolkata and going to Rishikesh!" I replied pointedly. He must have been in his fifties, but yet seemed fitter than NBA basketball players.

"Aashoon! Aashoon! (Come, come) Rishikesh is still some distance from here," he said, pulling a wooden chair and sitting next to us.

"Wow, you seem to know Bengali well," I said, pleasantly surprised when Sardarji spoke in Bengali. In my last one year, I had learnt five words of Bengali, that too only the bad ones.

"My customers come from all over the country and I pick up new languages conversing with them. Would you believe if I tell you that I can speak nine Indian and two foreign languages?" he said, grinning, while Raja and I looked at one another in astonishment.

"What should I serve you today? Our sarson ka saag and makke ki roti are the hot selling items during this season," said Sardarji.

Soon a young boy at the dhaba brought us sarson ka saag, black daal and makke ki roti, and placed it on our table. I looked at the steaming hot sarson ka saag. It had enough white butter in it to keep a ship afloat. Having heard so much about this dish, I tasted a spoonful of it and it just melted in my mouth. 'Awesome' was the word. We lost count of the makke ki rotis we had between us. With so much of food inside us, we burped aloud.

"Twenty-five rotis between the both of you tells me that you have liked the food" said Sardarji, grinning. "You have a long way from here to Rishikesh. Why don't you try our lassi now? It will settle all the food that you have eaten."

"Sorry boss, your food has been really delicious, but there is no place in my tummy for lassi!" I said, politely refusing.

"I think I will risk it. The sarson ka saag was marvelous and imagine how good the lassi will be!" said Raja. Despite a stomach full of lunch, he still wanted to have lassi.

"Boys, let me tell you, the lassi in our dhaba is free. You are here for the first time so you might not know, but it is our tradition to offer free lassi to all the customers since the last forty years, whether you eat for ten rupees or one thousand rupees!" said Sardarji with his ever smiling face.

That was slightly odd. Offering lassi to anyone who ate irrespective of the bill amount appeared to be illogical. It would incur huge losses for Sardarji without him realizing it.

"Wouldn't you be losing money if every customer has free lassi?" I argued.

"You have the lassi first and then we will talk about the profit and loss model," said Sardarji, carrying the same charm. Sardarji gestured and the same boy shortly returned with two lassis in large brass glasses.

"This dhaba is now forty years old. When my father opened it, there were around ten more food joints that started the very same year. Unfortunately, all of them closed as they couldn't run the business, but ours continued to flourish. From one table to start with, we have grown to a hundred tables today," said Sardarji with his face beaming with pride.

"That is good to know, but what has it got to do with the free lassi?" I asked, getting impatient. I was tired from a long journey, but his story seemed interesting.

"My father always wanted to give back from the profits that he would make from his business and that is how he started serving free lassi to all the customers here, irrespective of their food bills. From that day until today, this tradition of free lassi has continued and will continue as well. One day, when he was very unwell and he knew that his time was up, he called me and said that he wanted to tell me one secret," said Sardarji.

Raja and I were paying attention to his story.

"He said the art of living is actually the art of giving. He also mentioned that that whatever is selflessly given to the creatures of God, without expecting any profit, actually comes back ten times over," said Sardarji with conviction on his face.

"How would you prove that free lassi is the prime reason behind the success of your business?" I asked inquisitively. Being an engineering student, trying to find logic for everything was in my blood.

"If you ask me to prove what I believe, maybe I can't. You may have a few beliefs as well, but if I ask you to prove them, you may spend your entire life without being able to do so. My father before passing away also said that the human mind is so myopic that it will never be able to logically link or prove that selfless giving comes back ten times over, but this is how the energies of our universe work," said Sardarji patiently.

I did not have anything to counter this. Isn't it true that we can't prove most of our beliefs? In fact, most of our life is around beliefs, isn't it?

Soon, we were back in our Innova and we resumed our journey to Rishikesh. Sardarji's words were continuously tingling in my mind. He had mentioned that anything selflessly served to the creatures of God came back ten times over. He had also said that not all things can be proved with logic, but it worked for him. I tried connecting all his statements, all the things that he had mentioned and something topical came out that I had been striving for long. Logic, or medical science if you would, seemed to have closed all doors for Sarangi, and here Sardarji said that not all the things in life could be explained by logic and science. Not only that, he had given an example of himself that his business prospered while his competition dissolved. Was this the reason that my grandfather asked me to stop by this dhaba? His story had a very relevant lesson, but how was it related to Sarangi's battle for life, I could not understand.

We reached Rishikesh at six in the evening. It had become slightly dark and the stars were almost out, but the cab driver did not have difficulty in locating the place as I was guiding him with the print out of maps.

"Stop here. This seems to be the place where we have to go," I said, instructing the driver.

I stepped out of the car and felt an unusual chill in the air. It occurred to me that the Ganges was flowing nearby. It was a big white-coloured building and the sign board in front of us indicated left for reception and we walked in that direction. Soon we were greeted by a person at the reception.

"You are Sarthak, and you've come from Kolkata to meet Guruji, right?" said the person. With him knowing my name and where I had come from, it was easy to guess that my grandfather must have spoken to him before my arrival. The mysterious person whom my grandfather wanted me to meet was a 'guru', a saint. That felt slightly absurd to me. How would a spiritual guru help save Sarangi who was battling terminal stage leukemia? I wondered if my grandfather had sent me to a totally irrelevant place or did he not understand my problem at all. Maybe age was catching up with him. I had always hated these frauds and good for nothing, self-proclaimed saints.

"Yes, I am Sarthak and he is my friend Raja. Can we meet Guruji now?" I asked, getting restless. I thought I'd meet him, even though prima facie, it didn't look like if he could solve my problem.

"Not today. You can only meet him if you have prior appointment, but I can try to arrange a meeting tomorrow. You can spend your night here in our guesthouse," said the reception person.

I was frustrated at not being able to see him, but the next day did not seem too late. I nodded.

"Is this your first time in Rishikesh? If yes, I would recommend you go and do some sightseeing. Take this map. It has details of good tourist places that you can see, but you have to rush as it is getting dark," said the receptionist handing me a tourist map of Rishikesh.

"Can I ask you something, if you don't mind please?" I asked. I had a thousand one-sided questions running in my mind on this cryptic 'guru' ever since my grandfather had mentioned him to me.

"Yes, sure," he nodded though he was slightly taken aback.

"How old is your Guruji?" I asked, as my grandfather mentioned he was young when he was helped by the Guru. Hearing this, the reception person had a silent smile on his face.

"This question has been asked by a lot of people and therefore I will narrate a short story which I narrated to them as well. Guruji visits America very often as he has many followers there. That fan following includes lots of doctors too. Given various theories about Guruji's age, they requested for some fitness tests to be done on him and Guruji happily agreed," said the reception person.

"And what were the results?" I asked, getting restless.

"Well, the reports said that his lungs were found to be as strong as a twenty-five-year-old Olympian, his eye sight being 6/6 and blood pressure 120/80."

"Really?" I asked astonished. This was a very high level of fitness for a person of any age, let alone the Guru.

"He hasn't sneezed in the last fifty years, let alone catch a cold or any infection," continued the reception person. I listened in amazement as he described the Guru.

"No one knows his actual age, but the popular belief here is that he is as old as this ashram," he said firmly, and looking straight into my eyes.

"Okay, how old is this ashram then?" I asked curiously.

"People in Rishikesh say that the foundation of this ashram was laid in the nineteenth century, somewhere around 1865. If that is assumed to be true, this ashram and Guruji both are around a hundred and fifty years old," the receptionist said.

"What?" I said gob-struck. I looked at Raja whose mouth was wide open.

With all those difficult to believe facts, we came out of the building to start our sightseeing albeit the darkness descending upon the town. Raja sat in the Innova while I dialled my grandfather's number to confirm the things that the receptionist had told us. I was surprised when my grandfather told me that he hadn't spoken to anyone at the Rishikesh ashram about my coming. If my grandfather did not tell the Guru, then how did the receptionist know my name and my purpose of coming? Were we living in the material age or were we dreaming? With all the incidents that had happened in the last fifteen minutes, he was turning out to be the most inexplicable man I was going to meet.

With the tourist maps in hand, we started our sightseeing trip in Rishikesh and the first tourist place was Triveni Ghat. It is the bank of the holy river Ganges that draws thousands of devotees every evening who worship the Ganges. I went a few steps into the river till the water was knee deep. Doesn't silently flowing water touching you have its own way of soothing things and calming the rush of life? Soon, the prayers at Triveni Ghat started and it was out of the world to watch such a crowd sing in chorus. If God was anywhere on earth, it was this place. I loved the bustle and the activity of the streets, and the small tea shops on the roadside. The evening had turned into a starry night and the next place I wanted to see was the Lakshmana Jhoola. It is a swinging bridge built on top of the river Ganges where you could experience a divine breeze every time. The blue water of the Ganges had turned black, imitating the colour of sky. It was a celestial experience. Soon, we were back at the ashram and the receptionist showed us the room where we were supposed to spend our night before our meeting with the Guru the next day. While going to bed, the Guru's age of one hundred fifty years was on my mind a great deal. Having lungs as strong as an Olympian and not sneezing in the last fifty years was way too difficult to believe. What would this person look like? In my entire quest to find someone who could bring back Sarangi to life, he was coming extremely close. I went to sleep that night, hoping that God would be kind to Sarangi.

✠

The next morning, the room's doorbell rang and it was the reception guy ready to take us to the cryptic Guru.

"I wanted to ask you something since yesterday. How did you know my name and that I would be coming?" I asked him. This question had puzzled me the entire night.

"Guruji himself told me a day before your arrival," said the receptionist, walking through the corridor alongside us.

"Well, how did your Guru know that I would be here? I spoke to my grandfather and he told me that he hadn't spoken to you or the Guru?" I asked, trying to catch up with his fast pace.

"Wait until your meeting with Guruji!" said the receptionist, with a quizzical smile on his face, but chosing not to answer my question.

The three of us crossed the white coloured ashram building and walked towards the small apartments that were fenced by lots of plantation. Between the ashram and the apartments, there was a stadium-sized ground that had hundreds of people sitting in it. They were patiently listening to someone who was delivering a lecture from a distant stage.

"Who are these people, and who is this person on the stage?" I asked, walking along with the receptionist.

"These are Guruji's followers who have come from all over the world to listen to his preaching," said the receptionist.

"From all over the world to listen to his sayings. But why?" I asked, puzzled.

"They also have problems like you, where no solution seems to be at hand," he said with conviction in his voice. I had no answer to his statement. He seemed to know all about my case too and I had no clue how. Bewildered, I looked at the other side of the ground. A big crowd was sitting on the ground with food being served to them by volunteers.

"And all this food, where does it come from and who are the people cooking and serving?" I asked, still fazed.

"Volunteers! We have many of them who donate food, money and time as charity to us. We, on a monthly basis, publish what we need on our website and in no time, we receive our needs from our well-wishers around the world," said the receptionist, calmly walking with me.

"And if I may know the logic behind all this?" asked a curious Raja. Every engineering student tries to find logic in anything that is being said and done.

"Well, it is a discussion worth days but since you have asked, let me explain it to you. The human mind is extremely myopic and always searches for logic in their acts and selfishly focuses on the 'me' first. This is where most of the problems start manifesting. The secret to happiness doesn't lie in holding or piling on things, but in letting them go, by giving them to those who are needy. The human mind will never be able to see that. If you give selflessly without expecting anything in return, you end up attracting and attaining at least ten times more," he said subtly, but with deep faith.

"And never ever try to associate this selfless giving with logic. It is a supreme act that one can do and hence it is beyond logic. No matter how hard you may try, you will never be able to connect them or prove it!" said the receptionist with a grin.

Dumbfounded, Raja and I looked at one another. The reception guy and the Sardarji at the Dhaba had the same things to say. Even their words matched. Was it a coincidence? Were these divine signals of some sort to save Sarangi? As they say, don't dismiss coincidences; they are signals.

We shortly reached the dimly-lit room where we were supposed to have our meeting with the cryptic Guru. Truth be told, I was nervous to the core to meet my last and final hope, as Sarangi had very little time left in this one sided battle. I also wanted to know, being a hundred and fifty years or even more, what had he done to defy aging and beat the cycle of life and death? I walked with my fingers crossed in hopes of seeing some light after days of wasted struggle.

"You sit here and Guruji will sit opposite you," said the receptionist, instructing us to sit on a small green cotton carpet spread on the floor. Soon, I saw a pair of legs taking off wooden sandals and placing them outside the room. I had read about those wooden sandals in my history book in my childhood and they were known as '*khadaoun*'. They were sandals to be worn by the people of extraordinary intellect. The room had little visibility and one could hardly see things beyond five feet. With that 'someone' coming inside the room, it suddenly appeared lit up. I tried looking at the person who had entered the room, but couldn't as the room was filled with white light. It was so bright as if there were a thousand suns in the sky at once.

Raja and I continued sitting there and the brightness eventually dimmed. The Guru was in front of us. He stood erect with long black hair, and appeared ideal in every respect. His physique displayed no signs of aging. He was dressed in plain white coloured clothes with sandalwood paste applied on his forehead. His face exuded the calm that comes from knowing it all. One sight of him, and I felt the peace of another world entering me, and strangely, my fears for Sarangi's condition subsided. It occurred to me that for the first time in the last two months, I didn't feel nervous and tired; such was his presence.

He sat opposite to us, locked himself in the lotus pose and closed his eyes.

"I had met your grandfather about seventy-three years ago. I know he is doing well but was unwell a few days back," he said with his eyes closed. I felt embarrassed as I had called my grandfather but had not inquired about his health.

"I am also aware that your girlfriend Sarangi is left with limited time," he said with his eyes closed. He seemed to have gone into some sort of a trance. At this point in time, I did not want to rack my brains on how he knew my name, my grandfather, and Sarangi, but wanted to know his recommendations on ways to save Sarangi. He was by far the most unexplainable personality I had ever met.

"For your friend Sarangi, I have three things to tell you. Do not have your mind wandering in confusion like it is now and listen carefully to what I have to say," he said, with his eyes closed and a mesmerizing aura on his face. He seemed to have read my mind.

"Everything that we see, observe, sense and do is all pre-scripted. The future is pre-scripted as well. The next page of this invisible script of destiny gets unfolded in front of us and we simply play to its tunes, perceiving that we are the doers when we are not. If Sarangi has been facing this ill-fated condition of life and death, it had been, unfortunately, scripted even before she was born. And if the script says she is destined to die in the next two months, no one can change it...neither Dr. Pratik, nor Dr. Biswas, me or you," the Guru said unfazed, with his eyes still closed. He was still in a trance. He seemed to know it all as he mentioned the names of Dr. Pratik and Dr. Biswas. This time I was not surprised but pained. With my grandfather's assurance and the events that I had been witnessing in the last two days, I had high hopes from this Guru. He was the single reason for my travel from Kolkata. Hearing him saying that no one could save Sarangi, I was devastated. I was about to experience a black out in my mind before he gave his second recommendation.

"My second advice to you is that though the future is pre-scripted, it does not mean that we cannot change the script!" said the Guru firmly. His eyes were still closed. With his every statement, it was becoming more mysterious, more complex and difficult to comprehend. It occurred to me that his second statement was in complete contradiction with the first one. Firstly, he had said it was all destined and then he mentioned that it could be changed. It brought a ray of sunshine, but some confusion too.

"First you say the future is pre-scripted and then you say it can be changed. Sarangi is inches away from the inevitable and I have come here with a lot of faith," I said in pain. Truth be told, the last three months had been trying and my soul was injured badly seeing Sarangi deteriorate into a vegetative state.

He did not answer my question as he seemed to be in a trance and in a different plane altogether.

"My third advice is the sacred unknown secret that all the objects in the universe obey. When you start giving selflessly to the others, good fortune starts coming back to you ten-folds. Therefore, if you want to save Sarangi, save or help save someone in similar conditions of life and death with your full force. The moment you do so, I will come and save Sarangi myself, no matter how advanced the disease, no matter what medical science says or Dr. Biswas says!" said the Guru with his eyes still closed in a trance.

I was knocked out. I was witnessing an event that seemed outside the range of scientific explanation, absolutely paranormal. Let alone finding hope for Sarangi in the last three months when top doctors had ruled out any chances of Sarangi's survival, here was a person confidently claiming that he would save Sarangi himself. How he would save Sarangi I had no clue, but there was no reason to distrust him. He was my grandfather's recommendation.

After he gave his three recommendations, he murmured something and I tried listening to them attentively.

"I am the taste of water; the light of the sun and the moon; I am the sound in ether and ability in man. I am the universal father, mother, granter of all, grandfather, and object of knowledge; purifier, the holy syllable 'Om', and three fold sacred love," he uttered softly. I had no clue of what was happening around me. It was a totally new dimension, new plane, a new sight that defied science and logic.

Shortly, he opened his eyes but remained locked in the lotus pose. We thanked him and came out of the room, while an English couple, who was waiting outside came inside.

"Hope the meeting with Guruji was a good one," said the receptionist with an amused smile on his face. I did not say anything as I was still trying to comprehend his recommendations. Guru's saying had no connection with Sarangi's cure but at times you have to trust your karma, gut, instinct, call it whatever you may. What else could have I done, when Sarangi was a few days away from the inevitable with no hope in sight. We sat inside the Innova and started our journey back from Rishikesh to Delhi. After a few hours, we were at New Delhi airport to catch our Indigo flight to Kolkata.

"Don't talk about this incident to anyone. No one will believe us and people would think we were either on drugs or have gone crazy," I said to Raja, when he was getting off the yellow taxi near his house.

"And what do I tell my father now about how I fared in the interview? The tall story that you told him, asshole," asked a nervous Raja.

"Say that as usual the interview panelist had low IQ and couldn't understand your intelligent answers. Before he could reject you, you rejected him!" I said, closing the taxi door and smiling.

"Dog…" said Raja, grinning.

It was a transcendental experience meeting the Guru. How would those three sayings help Sarangi come out of the clutches of death, no one knew. It won't be too long before the next chapter reveals whether my stars had started to align and if I could feel their pulse. Who won in this roll of dice between me and Sarangi's destiny? Did I manage to beat this mighty script of destiny or did Sarangi succumb to the design of powerful destiny? Be with me.

Taming the Invisible
Script of Destiny

⌘

I was back from my meeting with the Guru. In the meantime, another week passed and by this time, Sarangi had become completely bedridden, troubled with major pains and seizures. Doctors had prescribed stronger doses of painkillers and sedatives to control them. As per them, it was just a matter of time, before it would be all over.

Guru had said if I could save someone in these conditions of life and death, he would come himself. Where could I locate someone like that? Next day, I went to office with my hair grown and unshaven. Someone has said it right, misfortune tames human minds. For the whole day, I did not do any work but sat in front of my computer wondering how the Guru would save Sarangi if I was able to help save someone in a similar condition of life and death. Like a panther in the cage, my mind had started to go up and down, looking forward for constant action. I had no other choice but to trust that the dots would somehow get connected. My deep thoughts were interrupted by a phone call from Sarangi's dad.

"Sarthak, I am urgently stuck in some work. I realized that Sarangi's medicines will be over by evening. Can I send you the prescription in an email so that you can get it renewed by Dr. Biswas and then buy the medicines?" said Sarangi's father, sounding fatigued. The struggle to save Sarangi had worn him out.

Shortly, I had the email from Sarangi's father in my inbox. I took a print out in my office and drove straight to Dr. Biswas's chamber.

"You are Sarthak and need a prescription renewal! Correct?" asked the doctor, "Sarangi's father had called me."

"How is the patient doing?" he asked, renewing the prescription.

I kept mum as I had nothing positive to stay. He too understood that and did not ask any further. I came out with the renewed prescription in my hand. Since it was an oncology department, the people waiting outside were either patients themselves or their relatives. While stepping out of the clinic, it occurred to me that someone had captured my attention. I turned back and saw a man holding a little boy in his arms. His wife was standing nearby. The couple must have been in their thirties and the little boy must have been four years old. They didn't seem to be too well off either. Since it was an oncology department, it was easy to guess that one of them was a cancer patient. My mother used to say that if you know someone who has cancer, try not to look at them with sad eyes. Treat them with empathy, with a little extra love.

I walked a few steps and stood close to them trying to listen to their conversation on the pretext of talking to someone over phone. In the next half an hour, I could gather that they were from Chapra district in Bihar. The man was an auto rickshaw driver and the sole bread earner of the family. They were concerned about how they would afford the high cost of treatment. I remembered the Guru's third saying. The situation at hand appeared to be a perfect shot and the dots seemed to be getting connected.

"Kitna paisa chahiye aapko?" I asked the couple.

The couple was blown away by the direct question from me, a stranger to them.

"Sorry, do we know you?" asked the little boy's father, confused.

"Consider me a friend! Just wanted to know who the patient among you is and how much money do you guys need?" I asked trying to make conversation.

Though I had overheard their discussion, I still couldn't make out who the patient was amongst the three of them. Ever since Sarangi was diagnosed with leukemia, I had started to treat strangers with compassion. We have no idea of the battles they fight in their lives.

The couple was hesitant at the outset, but shortly opened up. As they say, people with common problems find a friend in one another.

The little boy, who was sleeping in his father's arms was the patient. He was diagnosed with liver cirrhosis, another example of God's cruel script for one more of his creations. While this was bad news, it was not so shattering either. His liver cirrhosis had been detected in the initial stages and was curable with medicines. The little boy's father, however, needed three lakh rupees for the boy's treatment which he did not have.

"Even if I sell my auto rickshaw, and my wife's silver jewellery, I will hardly be able to gather fifty thousand. The hospital won't start the treatment unless they have received the full payment of three lakhs in advance," he said, sounding beaten.

"I cannot see something bad happening to my child. He is my only son and he has not done any wrong to anyone," said the woman, weeping.

The little boy still had a chance as his condition wasn't life-threatening. What wrong had Sarangi done to deserve such a fate? A thousand questions, but there weren't any answers. I also came to know that this family had come to the hospital a week ago only and his cirrhosis was detected this morning. Wasn't this a divine signal? Weren't the dots getting connected? The couple needed money and I could give it to them. By doing so, I would have helped save the little boy and the Guru promised that he would come himself to save Sarangi, right?

"Guys, just be here and I will be back with the money in twenty minutes!" I said. The couple looked astounded.

"Don't bother about returning the money! I don't need it," I said patting the little boy's head. I just wanted to tell his parents that when man closes one door, God opens two. While the boy's father couldn't stop thanking me, the mother was in tears. There is sacredness in tears. They are not a mark of weakness, but that of strength. I walked towards an ICICI bank branch opposite to the hospital.

"Sir, the maximum that you could withdraw is two lakh sixty thousand. Since it is not a zero balance account, you would need to keep ten thousand in the account!" said the bank teller. While promising the couple, it slipped from my mind that I had spent more than two lakhs for purchasing my Santro a few months back and the balance had dipped down to two lakh sixty thousand. I was short of fifty thousand as the bank needed a minimum balance of ten thousand.

"Give me two lakh fifty thousand. Let me withdraw whatever maximum I can," I said, filling the aforesaid amount in the withdrawal slip and giving it to the teller. While she was counting the cash, I tried calling Raja and Ankur, knowing well that they wouldn't be able to help as they did not have any jobs yet.

With that money in hand, I entered the hospital and walked towards the couple. I realized that my phone had been vibrating for the last few minutes. I looked at the number that was flashing and it couldn't have been worse timing. It was from KC Agarwal, the same jeweller who had given me the ring based on my promise to return the money the next day. With the devastating news of Sarangi's illness, I had forgotten my own self, let alone returning the money for his ring. I was a liar in his eyes. And a liar is worse than a thief.

"You thug…! It was my fault that I trusted you on that day, despite my staffs' warning," shouted KC, hopping mad. "I have seen you at the entrance of Goodland Hospital. Don't even try to move an inch, else I will call the police and report to your HR as well," said the spiked KC over phone.

Before I could think of anything, KC in his white kurta pajama and a heavy gold chain around his neck was in front of me with four goons.

"Smart move, dude! First, win my trust with a nicely cooked up story and then vanish into thin air with the ring! But what you forgot is that I am a Marwari businessman. If I know how to give, I know fully well how to extort it as well," he said, maddened and taking a step towards me with two of his men.

"I need my thirty-five thousand right away. I also know you have more in your bag as I saw you withdrawing more than two lakhs," said an aggravated KC.

"Thirty-five thousand! But the ring was for fifteen thousand, then why the additional twenty thousand?" I queried.

"That is the penalty for the delay in payment," said KC sounding exasperated. He was accompanied by four well-built men and I was all by myself. There was no way I could have resisted or refused.

I had two options: either I could return his thirty-five thousand or I could turn defiant and refuse him the money as I was still short of fifty thousand. None of them was ideal, as the first one would prove me a liar and the second one, a fraud. But then there was a third option too: explaining the entire situation and asking for the remaining fifty thousand. I didn't realize that I had taken more than a minute thinking about the options.

"My money, boss! The last thing I want is my men to batter you here and then hand you over to the police," said KC, intimidating me.

"Here is your money!" I said, taking out one bundle of five hundred rupee notes from the bag and handing it to him. "This is fifty thousand and not thirty-five. I apologize for the delay and hence the additional fifteen thousand."

Unperturbed, he picked up the bundle fast and started counting the notes. When he found out that there was indeed an additional fifteen thousand, he appeared in a better frame of mind.

"Can I tell you a small incident if you have a minute? You have got more money than you asked for anyway," I asked pointedly, now that I had made up for the delay with the extra payment.

"What new story do you want to tell me now?" he said, appearing less infuriated.

"Let us get to a side. The story will take a few minutes," I requested and he reluctantly nodded. Once bitten and twice shy, KC looked skeptical. I had to think of where to start. So I took the plunge and threw all that I had on the table. I narrated the conditions in which I had borrowed the ring and proposed to Sarangi, how we had tried all the options out but medical science seemed to have closed all its doors. I also told him how crushed and desperate I felt when all the doors were closed. I narrated how I met this Guru in Rishikesh. I told him about the couple and my intent to help them, the shortage of funds and how this money would possibly help to save the little one. It is astonishing how one recollects such things. This story leapt out as if it was embedded in my soul. KC was nothing short of stumped on hearing all this. He stared at me for more than a few seconds.

"I am short of fifty thousand and if you can lend me fifty thousand more, the boy and hopefully Sarangi, as per the Guru's words, will be saved. Take my iPhone and my car keys," I said handing over my phone and car keys to him. History had repeated itself. I had a sense of déjà vu of my previous visit to his shop.

"Even if I believe your story, how would helping this boy save Sarangi?" he asked, puzzled. He was baffled when I told him the Guru's three sayings.

"If you ask me to prove what I believe, I can't. It may be true for you also. You may also have a few beliefs but if I ask you to prove them, you may spend your entire lifetime without being able to do that," I said what the dhabawala Sardarji and the receptionist had told me.

KC looked at the little boy, who was sleeping calmly in his father's arms with a faith that nothing would happen to him. He appeared frozen for a moment and what happened in the next five minutes, would stun everyone around.

"Akbar! Go to my car and get my black bag from there!" said KC to one of his men standing nearby.

"What boss?" asked Akbar. Even he could not comprehend KC's change of mind.

"I said go to the car and get my black bag from the backseat," he said, more sternly this time. While Akbar went out to get the bag, the couple with the little boy stood at a distance. They had no clue about the long conversation KC and I were having. Soon, Akbar was back.

"Here is one lakh to help save this boy. I don't know if your story is true or not, but my gut tells me to help this little boy. You can return the money for the ring when your salary comes in after seven days, but I don't want the money for the boy to be returned," he said, taking out two bundles of five hundred rupee notes. He handed me my fifty thousand back too.

"I need to go for a business meeting, but if you need more money for this little boy or Sarangi, you have my number," KC said, putting his hand on my shoulder. I thanked him for his gratitude. Someone has said it right – accidents in life at times end up in building the best relationships.

"Marwaris have hearts too, my friend," he said, putting his hand on my shoulder and I spotted a teardrop in his left eye. I hugged KC and he hugged me back.

"Keep the three lakhs and start the treatment for your son. Here is my office card that has my phone number. If there is anything that you need in the city, give me a call," I said, reassuring the couple who had been distressed a great deal, but looked visibly relieved.

"You have come to us as a God to save our child. Since the last five minutes, I have been pinching myself to make sure this is not a dream," said the mother of the little boy. The tears were not stopping from her eyes. As they say, connections are made with the heart, not the tongue.

"The little fellow will be fine soon!" I said, hiding the tears in my eyes too. Tears shed for another person are not a sign of weakness. They are the sign of a pure heart. In the meantime, the little boy had got up from his nap and saw his emotional mother.

"Ma! Why are you crying? Look, Papa has started to smile now after months!" said the little boy innocently.

Is it always curtains when the physician says it is over? The answer is no. Unless God says no, it is never over. And you will find that out in a minute.

I drove back home with a sense of satisfaction of saving someone's life with my effort but the bigger question was still unanswered. How would saving the life of the little boy save Sarangi? The Guru had said he himself would come to save Sarangi, but he was nowhere in sight. What did he mean when he said he himself would come? Time was running out faster than ever before and we were hardly left with a few weeks.

✠

The next day, I visited Sarangi's home after office. She was lying on the bed, looking unwell but awake.

She looked at me and smiled, but couldn't speak. I just held her hand to tell her that I was with her.

"All will be fine soon. I have met someone who can help us," I said, gently stroking her forehead.

Disturbed and pained, I came back home wondering how on earth would the Guru come and save Sarangi. Would he come himself or send someone? Sometimes life is too hard to be alone and sometimes it is best to be left alone. I came home, ate a packet of Maggi and tried sleeping on the bed but sleep wasn't coming to me anytime soon. There was a lot of turbulence that I was starting to feel inside. As the wise say, only after the storm is over, comes the sunshine. Somehow it occurred to me that I had not spoken to my father for a very long time. There were mistakes on my part too. I did not even bother to inform him when I started out from Delhi after I got the job in Kolkata. I decided to call him up the next morning.

"Dad," I said guilt ridden, and there was a long silence on the line. There is nothing that moves a loving father's soul quite like his child's voice.

"Do you realize we haven't spoken for a long time," I said, feeling saddened. If I was the culprit, wasn't he too?

"I am glad we are talking again," he choked after having received a call from his son after so many months.

I still had faint memories of the good times spent with my father. Both of us would play in the backyard of our house when I was about four years old. While playing we would spoil the garden and my mother would get annoyed and say, "You are tearing up the grass".

My dad would reply, "I am not raising grass, I am raising a boy."

He however changed a lot when I went to school. All of a sudden, he did not have time for the family. No one knew why.

I narrated Sarangi's story to him though I did not tell him that she was my girlfriend. Some details best remain hidden.

During the course of our conversation, he mentioned an incident of twenty years ago when one of his friends had suffered an intense heart attack and was rushed to a leading cardiac care hospital in Delhi. Though the doctors operated upon him, they also predicted his remaining life span to be not more than six months. He then started an alternate line of treatment and managed to live a healthy life of nineteen years more, until dying his natural death at the age of eighty-seven.

"Another nineteen years, awesome! That is what I have badly wanted to hear since the last two months, someone who had defied medical science," I said, getting a kick. The news of someone challenging the rules of medical science had brought a ray of sunshine.

"That colleague of mine isn't any more but he had a son by the name of Amit Singh who was studying in IIT Delhi at that point in time. I however wouldn't know where Amit is today. If you can locate him, you will get all the details about the doctor who had treated his father and his whereabouts!" he said.

Locate a guy who used to study in IIT Delhi nineteen years ago? The irony of life is that before one challenge is resolved, another one pops up.

"Why didn't you tell me earlier? We could have saved Sarangi," came out the words from my wounded soul.

"Why didn't you call me earlier?" said an equally emotionally choked old father on the other side.

Though I did not tell my father about our relationship, he was mature enough to have guessed it by now. We disconnected shortly. My own father had been missing from my life and I could only hope that he would become a part of it again.

It was the time for the pedal to hit the metal. A Facebook search on 'Amit Singh, IIT Delhi' gave me a never-ending list of seventy-five Amit Singhs. With this long a list, finding out the right Amit Singh was going to be an uphill task, given the time in hand. I felt helpless but then there is no such thing as helplessness. It is just another way of giving up.

Dear Amit, if your father was a lieutenant in the Delhi army cantonment area in the 1990s, I need to talk to you urgently. Please let me know.

I typed the message and shot it to all the seventy-five Amit Singhs until three in the morning.

But was it possible to find out the needed Amit Singh in one go? Social networks though have undoubtedly connected the world like never before, but have raised the bar of trust too. What if the needed Amit Singh did not take the Facebook message seriously? I was treading on a very thin line. That night I went to bed hoping that the world would be kind to Sarangi. Next day, out of all the seventy-five Amit Singhs to whom I had sent the email, I got responses from two different Amit Singhs. The first one said that he sympathized with my friend's case but he was not the one whom I was looking for. I felt gutted. But then as they say, the solutions present themselves, when there seems no solution. The second email turned out to be the one I had been desperately waiting for. My job at that point in time was to speak to him at the earliest as Sarangi was left with miniscule time. Amit had been living in Minneapolis, United States of America, with his family for the last sixteen years. In the mail, he had shared his number and had requested to call the next day during evening time, which would be morning here. In life, one should never lose hope. Only when the sun goes down do the stars come out. I was starting to get a feeling that I was getting a handle on Sarangi's invisible script of destiny, which is part of the thinking behind the book you are holding.

The next day, I reached office early at seven in the morning when there was not even a soul around and dialled his number.

"Amit?" I asked.

"Yes, Sarthak, how are you doing?" he asked politely.

We connected as if we were destined to speak. Our conversation started and he told me the same story that my dad had told me. Amit's dad had suffered a massive heart attack and army doctors ruled out chances of survival unless he was to have a heart transplant. In the nineties, medical science in India was still underdeveloped to have full transplant facilities. Having given up all hope on the medical science, his dad had consulted an ayurvedic practitioner in Haridwar, a small city in northern India, close to Rishikesh. With the treatment of this practitioner, his dad not only fully recovered in three months, but went on to live for another nineteen years. The doctors were dumbfounded seeing the results. They wanted to know what his dad had done, but he did not reveal, as it was a condition put forward by the ayurvedic practitioner.

"Why are you telling me if that ayurvedic practitioner is not open to the idea of being known in public?" I asked, puzzled.

"If a broken promise can save someone's life, isn't it good?" he said.

"Thanks! Can you give me this ayurvedic practitioner's mobile number?" I asked, getting restless.

"I don't know his phone number as twenty years back there were no mobile phones. I can give you his postal address, better maybe a map for you to locate his house as the streets of Haridwar are rather confusing. Would that do?" he asked, and I agreed.

Thanking him, I disconnected the line. It was eight in the morning and by the time my watch showed nine, the email containing the map of the practitioner's postal address had landed in my inbox. Amit Singh was a good man. The good people we have known are those, who have known defeat, seen suffering and have found out their way from depth.

The wheel of fate seemed to have started moving again. I logged on to makemytrip.com and bought two tickets to Dehradun via Delhi – one for myself and one for Raja, who again had no clue that the next morning he would be up in the air. From Dehradun, I planned to take a cab to Haridwar. Haridwar is a beautiful city on the banks of the river Ganges that attracts hundreds of pilgrims, devotees, and tourists.

Our flight took off with a roaring sound and was soon up in the air. The sun was shining brightly and there was no turbulence in the air. Soon the airhostess started serving sandwiches and chocolates. Big impacts in life are not made by impulse but with the small things around us. How chocolates would prove to be life-saving, you will find out soon. Shortly thereafter, we were at the Indira Gandhi International Airport and boarded our connecting flight to Dehradun. The connecting flight just took thirty minutes to land at Jolly Grant Airport, an airport that is surrounded by lush green mountains. At the arrivals gate, we hired a taxi for the city of Haridwar and it drove through a picturesque landscape. We were soon in Haridwar. I was guiding the cab driver with directions to the ayurvedic practitioner's house using the map that Amit Singh had sent me.

"See the lane in front? You need to walk through that until you get to the last house on the street. That's what the map says," said the cab driver stopping in front of a narrow lane.

It was a bright day and Raja and I walked towards that long and isolated lane, crossing various houses of different shapes and sizes. Soon we reached the dead end of the road. In front of us was an old, yellow-coloured double-storied house. The house had a heavy wooden door and there were a few pair of shoes and sandals outside the house. One of the shoes caught my attention as it was a pair of khadaoun, similar to the ones I had seen at the Guru's place. Could they belong to the ayurvedic practitioner? Where there is great love, there are always miracles. I knocked at the door but no one answered for the next few minutes.

"Is any one at home?" I said, opening the door as much as I could as it was latched. Shortly, I heard some movement in the house and a little girl wearing a printed frock with two ribboned pony tails opened the door. She must have been no more than seven or eight years old.

"Yes, whom are you looking for?" the little girl asked. I was slightly taken aback at her directness and confidence.

"We want to meet the doctor, the ayurvedic practitioner. We have come from Kolkata, very far off," I said, getting fidgety.

"Doctor? Which doctor? There is no doctor here. Looks like someone has given you the wrong address," she said, trying to close the door.

And that answer from the girl had made me nervous, very nervous. Amit couldn't have given me the wrong address. Could it be that the ayurvedic practitioner was no longer alive and his family had shifted? There were always a thousand possibilities at that point of time in life. I felt the blues but I wasn't the one to give up.

"I got this address from someone whose father was treated by an ayurvedic physician residing at this address," I said with conviction.

"When was the treatment done for that patient?" asked the little girl assertively. She was too intelligent for her age.

"About twenty years back," I said, calculating from the top of my head.

"Okay, I got it now. You guys are talking about my grandfather, but I am sorry, unfortunately he doesn't see patients anymore. The last patient that he saw was around fifteen years back. Owing to his old age and ill-health, he can't even speak or listen," she said with sadness in her eyes.

That statement from the girl brought a ray of sunshine. The little girl unknowingly had given two answers to us; one, that we were at the right address and second, that the ayurvedic practitioner was alive. The next thing was to persuade the little girl to show Sarangi's report to the physician.

"Yes, he is the one whom I have come to see," I said regaining my composure.

"Didn't I tell you that he has stopped seeing patients? Lots of people like you come and request to see him, but I have to say no to all of them. I am sorry but you won't be able to show your patient to him," she said sounding rebellious.

Such a little girl and she knew how to say 'no' the hard way. Having crossed all the barriers to meet this doctor, convincing this little girl was proving to be a daunting task. We were treading on a thin line and I couldn't afford to go back without meeting this ayurvedic physician. I looked at Raja, who seemed to be in deep thought and that was an indication that he had an idea up the flagpole.

"Every girl likes chocolates. Would you like to have these?" asked Raja taking out the two Dairy Milk chocolates that the airhostess had handed to us in the flight. As they say, small things in life often become bigger than the great things.

There was a sudden pause in the little girl's continuous refusals and she looked puzzled. She appeared to be in a catch-22 situation of accepting chocolates and yet not allowing us to meet her grandfather. And this proved to be the turning point of the mind game. If you can win over someone's mind, you can win over anything in the world.

"See, if you allow us to meet your grandfather, you get a box full of these chocolates. One box has a dozen!" said Raja, placing an irresistible offer to the little girl. A chocolate says 'let's be friends' better than anything else.

"Is it a bribe to meet my grandfather?" she asked with a little grin.

"Yes, we are bribing a little girl, with a little love," I said, returning the smile.

"Okay, then wait here. I need to convince my grandfather as he hasn't seen anyone for ages, but I think if I recommend you, he won't refuse. Who is the patient among you and if you have got any reports, please give them to me. And by the way, my name is Aastha and not 'little girl'," she said before going inside.

"Here are the reports and the person who is unwell is in Kolkata," I said, handing her the file that had all of Sarangi's diagnostic reports. Aastha took the file inside just to come out in five minutes.

"He has agreed to meet you guys. Come, follow me!" she said walking towards a room. She did not have the reports in her hand this time and it was easy to guess that the reports were with her grandfather. The game was on. I was going to meet an ayurvedic physician who had beaten science at its own game. As I started walking towards the room, it occurred to me that I had travelled a long way to see this day.

We followed the little girl who took us to one small but well-lit room with a noisy fan running on moderate speed. We saw an elderly gentleman wearing a white kurta and dhoti, sitting on a wooden bed. There were sandalwood paste lines on his forehead. I looked around and noticed a copper jug filled with water on his bed side.

While Aastha gestured for us to sit on the wooden chairs opposite him, the elderly physician was busy writing something on a piece of paper that he soon handed to Aastha.

"I have gone through the reports. If you had come to me two months ago, this disease would have been completely curable. Anyone who remarked at that time that the disease is incurable does not understand the anatomy of the disease. The patient however is left with little life. Can she be cured, I can't guarantee as the medicine would take one month to start working. I would recommend that we start the medicine right away," said Aastha, reading out the words written by the ayurvedic practitioner.

For the first time, someone had said that she had a 'chance'. Hearing this, I cried without shame. Tears started coming out and I didn't attempt to stop them. My soul was injured and I wanted my tears to water it.

As per Dr. Biswas's calculation, Sarangi was left with no more than fifteen days, with the risk of a cardiac arrest any time. The medicine given by this practitioner would take a month to show any effect. I was up against all odds in life. A full blown battle was on between Sarangi and her destiny, moving fast towards the inevitable and me refusing to give up. We also had the blessings of the ayurvedic physician now. The only thing that we did not have by our side was time. We just did not have time.

Then there was a second piece of paper which Aastha read.

"Your medicines will be ready in the next one hour. Please start administering the doses from today itself and continue them for at least six months."

That was a confidence-building statement from the ayurvedic physician. We spent some time in the city, took a dip in the holy river Ganges and came back at two to collect the medicines.

"One last thing! Here is a sealed envelope that my grandfather wants you to open up after two months of treatment. Don't even attempt to open it before that time otherwise the medicines will stop working," she said, handing a tightly sealed envelope to me. While we were wondering how opening up the envelope would nullify the medicinal effect, she appeared lit up as she had got the box full of chocolates from Raja. What could have been inside that sealed envelope, which needed to be opened up only after two months? What did it have to do with Sarangi's treatment? To be honest, in the last one month, I had experienced a lot of paranormal events that were beyond my comprehension. There was no point in logically analyzing them now. We thanked the physician and Aastha and came back to our Innova.

Soon we were at the Dehradun airport and by the time the stars were out, we had reached Kolkata. I was nervous and tired from this ongoing battle, but this time we had something with us to fight against a declared victorious enemy. The ayurvedic physician had mentioned a minimum of a month for the medicines to work and unfortunately Sarangi did not have any more than fifteen days. Until this point, Sarangi's father had no clue of ayurvedic treatment and needed to be convinced. It wasn't going to be an easy task. Life had given me two options at this stage. Either I could start explaining my journey to Haridwar and try convincing him to give these medicines, but that could take a long time. The second option was to administer the medicines without his knowledge. I was in a big dilemma as it was a choice between a peaceful death and the rolling of a dice to revive Sarangi. With all these thoughts running in my mind and the bag of medicines in my hand, I got out of the cab and walked towards Sarangi's house. Between the cab and the house, something repetitively told me to stick to administering the medicines that the ayurvedic physician had given. I repeat, 'repetitively'.

I entered her house and it was completely silent with everyone sleeping. I went to Sarangi's room, lifted her head slightly and put four black coloured pills in her mouth with some water that was lying nearby. Once she had swallowed the pills, I placed her head back on the pillow. She gazed expressionless at me for a few seconds and closed her eyes. I was pained as she appeared unwell, very unwell.

The countdown had started and Sarangi's health was deteriorating day by day. I applied for loss of pay leave from my office to be with her all the time, to administer regular doses of those black coloured pills.

Sarangi was reduced to a vegetative state, declining day by day, and I was shattered seeing the despondent state of a once-vivacious and charming Sarangi. Life is half spent before we know what it is. The next two weeks passed and during this time, things went downhill. Sarangi would be unconscious all the time and would suffer major pains and seizures all throughout the day. It appeared to me that the new unproven line of treatment had landed her in some complicated mess.

One day, when my watch showed 11.00 p.m., fatigued and hopeless, I lay down on the sofa and started staring at the ceiling. While Sarangi did not even show any improvement, she was still alive. Dr. Biswas had cautioned that a cardiac arrest could occur any time and here fifteen days had passed by and no such thing had happened. Could we take that as an improvement? I was too unskilled to conclude that. Amidst thoughts running wild in my mind, the time had raced to 3.00 a.m. I felt sleepy and dozed off on the sofa itself. Her mother had cooked dinner for me but I did not feel like eating it. It was the fifteenth day, the doomsday that was predicted to be Sarangi's last day. At around six in the morning, I was awakened by a phone call. It was from Rajan.

"Sarthak, I know it is early in the day but we have a call with a Singapore client in the next fifteen minutes. I have mailed you a presentation. Do you think you can attend this call?" he asked impatiently.

I had been out of the office for more than two months now. Moreover, Rajan had been very kind in helping me with Sarangi's case, so I did not want to turn him down. Everyone in the house was fast asleep and I could take the call sitting in the hall.

"Yes, Rajan. I will," I said with sleepy eyes, but it was time to be awake. Soon our conference call with the Singapore client had started. No great innovative ideas have been born in conference calls but lots of foolish ideas have died there.

It was 7.30 a.m. and the call had been on for more than an hour. Having skipped dinner the previous night, I had started to feel hungry. To add to that, a bad headache had also started. For a moment, I thought of dropping the call and asking Sarangi's mother for breakfast, but it would have been very unprofessional to the customer and Rajan. In a dilemma of whether to continue with the call or to drop it, fifteen more minutes had passed by and my hunger was unendurable by now. Barely able to focus on the call, I finally decided to mute the phone and call Sarangi's mom to warm the previous night's dinner or give me something to eat. Deep in my thoughts, I was just about to press the mute button, when something on my left caught my attention. There was a hot cup of black tea, an omelette and an aaloo parantha on the side table. I muted the phone and took a sip from the cup and a big bite of the aaloo parantha. It tasted familiar, very familiar. The only people who knew that aaloo parantha and omelettes were my favourite food were my mother and Sarangi. It certainly could not have been my mother as she was in Delhi and I had spoken to her only the previous night. It was suddenly still and silent in the room, but there was something in that silence. As they say, silence is the language of God, all else is poor translation. I turned around and what I saw, I will still pinch myself to believe for ages to come. Take a guess.

It was Sarangi standing behind my back and smiling with tears rolling down her eyes. From being bedridden and in a vegetative state, she had gained enough energy to be able to get up and make breakfast for me. What could this have meant? That the medicine from the ayurvedic practitioner had started to work, fifteen days ahead of time? It was supposed to be the doomsday when she was to slip into a coma. This was nothing but a miracle. As they say, where there is great love, there are miracles. The Singapore call was finally over. It had become dark and had started raining heavily outside. Doesn't rain have a way of softening things, of calming the rush of life and healing the soul?

"Why are you sad, Sarthak?" she asked, hugging me and I hugged her for long while with tears rolling down our eyes. They were tears of joy.

"Mom, I am hungry. Give me some juice and corn flakes," she said going into her mom's room. For the first time in the last three months, she had asked for food and it was a clear indication that her body was starting to heal from within. Her parents couldn't believe what they were seeing and there were tears rolling down from her father's eyes too. A man's heart might be tough, but a father's heart is tender.

We hugged and the entire day passed in great positivity. In the evening, her tests were repeated and the reports that came out next day indicated a clear remission of the disease. And it called for opening of a bottle of champagne. If you believe something is true, and you weigh and measure the possibilities well, and you carry on with good faith, then your prediction will come true.

I took the reports to Dr. Biswas.

"I think there is something wrong with the reports. Maybe the blood sample got mixed with someone else's blood sample. Let me repeat the tests to be sure," said the doctor fazed.

History had repeated itself. There have been a few recurring themes in my life, and history getting repeated is one of them. When Sarangi's cancer was detected, I had my doubts about the test reports and now it was Dr. Biswas wanting to do the repeat tests. In the evening, the tests were done once again but nothing was different. As the wise say, three things cannot be hidden – the sun, the moon and the truth.

"I have never seen such a turnaround in my life. I am not sure how the reversal happened," said the doctor scratching his head.

"But I know," I said, but kept to myself. The faces of the Guru and the ayurvedic physician were running in my mind at that point in time.

It was time to thank a lot of people who had played an important role in making this possible; The Guru, my grandfather, the ayurvedic physician, KC, my dad, Amit Singh, my boss Rajan and two of my friends Raja and Ankur.

It was a time for celebration too. The Guru had indeed done what he had said he would, come himself to save Sarangi. I could clearly see all the dots getting connected. Sarangi's treatment continued for a few more months and she was back to her pink beautiful self. We started going for jogging to help her regain her fitness.

Few days later, I realized that the ayurvedic physician had also given one tightly sealed envelope and had strictly instructed me to open it after two months from the beginning of treatment. It was the fourth month. The medicines were continuing and presumably it was safe to open it now. What could have been in that envelope? A little anxious, I came back home early, closed the door and opened the envelope carefully. It had a small piece of paper with something written on both sides. The front side had the following text:

"Because you saved the little boy from Chapra from liver cirrhosis, I have come myself to save Sarangi."

I was simply speechless. How could the ayurvedic practitioner have known I had saved the little boy? Were he and the Guru one? My astonishment had no bounds.

I turned the paper around to read the text at the back of it.

"I am the taste of water, the light of the sun and the moon; I am the sound in ether and ability in man. I am the universal father, mother, granter of all, grandfather, and object of knowledge, purifier, the holy syllable 'Om', and three-fold sacred love."

They were the words that the Guru had murmured when I had gone to meet him. I stood there and suddenly it all seemed clear to me. The Guru and the ayurvedic doctor might have been two persons physically, but logically, were one. I read both sides of the paper again and my mind appeared free from all emotions. The peace of another world had entered in me. The Guru knew all that had happened in the past and what was going to happen. I came out into my balcony, looked at the sky; the stars were out. I bowed before the almighty and thanked the Guru. I had managed to reverse the script of Sarangi's destiny.

With the treatment continuing, Sarangi recovered fast and shortly resumed her job, but couldn't continue for long as we got married soon. NetCon had given me a project in London and we celebrated our honeymoon in the scenic beauty of Switzerland. A year later, our son was born and we named him Arjun.

Till this day, every night I have gone off to sleep with the Guru in my mind a great deal. When I look back, I still wonder how on earth did I pull it off. One day from London, I tried calling the Guru's reception and I was told that Guru had gone to the Himalayas with no one knowing his whereabouts. Subsequently, I called Aastha, the granddaughter of the ayurvedic practitioner and she told me that her grandfather had passed away a few days after my meeting with him. I still have that handwritten piece of paper from him, kept safely in my locker. I still at times, open it up and read it, but I don't try to associate any logic with it. There have been many miles, and now, many years, between me and the young boy Sarthak who had boarded the train to become a software professional in NetCon Consulting. This is the story of Sarthak who came in time to complete the work. But the story did not begin with the work, the work began with the story, and the journey of the two of us, Sarthak and Sarangi, became the story of our times.

Yours sincerely,
Sarthak Arora

At the end of my life, with just one breath left, if you come, I'll sit up and sing.

— *Rumi*

Upcoming title from the same author

Love, The Seventh Sense
When soulmates reunite

"Know therefore, that from a greater silence I shall return
Forget not that I shall come back to you.
A Little while, a moment of rest upon the wind,
And another woman shall bear me
If in the twilight of memory we should meet once more
We shall speak again together and you shall sing to me a deeper
song.
And if our hands should meet in another dream
We shall build another tower in the sky."

— *Khalil Gibran*

Bhushan is a bright but introvert computer engineer from an engineering college of renown in Delhi. He leaves behind the scars of all his father's abuses and a difficult childhood after his mother's demise when he joins a multinational in Chai Chee, Singapore.

Padma is from the same college and batch, equally bright, and much vibrant. She is all set to commence her Master's degree from the New York State University.

The memories of their eyes locking a thousand times without any words stay ripe in their hearts, though their love remains unconfessed. That's when Bhushan lands in New York on a work assignment, and professes his feelings over phone to Padma and both of them are predictably thrilled.

It is September 2011. He is in the lift carrying a bouquet of red roses. She is impatiently waiting at the reception of the 61st floor of World Trade Center…their hearts beating fast.

Moments before they meet, the World Trade Center is hit by a plane in a terrorist attack. Bhushan dies in the lift; Padma's body isn't found.

Will their story remain incomplete? Or will the soulmates find a way to reunite?

Witness a heart-stopping and soul-stirring narration, subtly conveying that soulmates travel the heavenly dimension of space and time to be with one another.